"Lizzy Sawyer Never Had Any Children!" Judd Insisted.

"She most certainly did. I have the papers to prove it. See? 'William Leighton Sawyer, born June 14, 1890, Oklahoma Territory. Son of Mary Elizabeth Sawyer.' He's my great-grandfather, and while he might be old, he's still very much alive!"

Judd caught Callie's arm and pulled her toward him. "You're a reporter, aren't you?" he asked suspiciously.

"A reporter? I don't know what you're talking about—"

"You came to find me, didn't you? Look me in the eye and tell me you've never heard of Judd Barker."

"No, I've never heard of—" She stiffened as the name clicked a hidden memory—one of headlines with the name in bold, dark type. And that was when she knew she could be in trouble.

Dear Reader,

This month we're filled with fabulous heroes, delightful babies, tie-in stories and a touch of the magical!

The MAN OF THE MONTH, *Mr. Easy*, is from one of your favorites, Cait London, who once again spins a love story in her own special way.

Next, we have *babies*. First, in *The Perfect Father*, another installment in the FROM HERE TO MATERNITY series by Elizabeth Bevarly, and next in Karen Leabo's wonderful *Beach Baby*.

For those of you who have been looking for the next episode of Suzanne Simms's HAZARDS, INC. series, look no more! It's here with *The Maddening Model*.

Peggy Moreland brings us a hero with a mysterious past—and a heroine with a scandalous ancestress—in *Miss Lizzy's Legacy*. And don't miss the very special *Errant Angel* by award-winning author Justine Davis.

This month—as with every month—if you want it special, sexy and superb, you'll find it…in Silhouette Desire.

Happy reading!

Lucia Macro
Senior Editor

Please address questions and book requests to:
Silhouette Reader Service
U.S.: 3010 Walden Ave., P.O. Box 1325, Buffalo, NY 14269
Canadian: P.O. Box 609, Fort Erie, Ont. L2A 5X3

PEGGY MORELAND
MISS LIZZY'S LEGACY

SILHOUETTE *Desire*®
Published by Silhouette Books
America's Publisher of Contemporary Romance

For my grandparents Jesse and Audra Admire, who
gave me my Oklahoma roots. Thanks for sharing with
me your love for the country, and by example, your
strength of character, your integrity and the joy
derived from simple things.

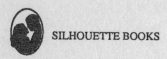 SILHOUETTE BOOKS

ISBN 0-373-05921-3

MISS LIZZY'S LEGACY

Copyright © 1995 by Peggy Bozeman Morse

Books by Peggy Moreland

Silhouette Desire

A Little Bit Country #515
Run for the Roses #598
Miss Prim #682
The Rescuer #765
Seven Year Itch #837
The Baby Doctor #867
Miss Lizzy's Legacy #921

PEGGY MORELAND

published her first romance with Silhouette in 1989. She's a natural storyteller with a sense of humor that will tickle your fancy, and Peggy's goal is to write a story that readers will remember long after the last page is turned. Winner of the 1992 National Reader's Choice Award and a 1994 RITA finalist, Peggy frequently appears on bestseller lists around the country. A native Texan, she and her family live in Round Rock, Texas.

Dear Reader,

Many times a story idea is spawned from a setting. Such is the case with *Miss Lizzy's Legacy*. Several years ago, I visited Guthrie, Oklahoma, and visited the Blue Bell Saloon and Miss Lizzie's. Once a bordello, the upstairs above the Blue Bell has been renovated into a collection of antique, art and gift shops and affectionately named Miss Lizzie's Bordello. I found the entire concept, as well as the speculation concerning Miss Lizzie, intriguing, and allowed my imagination to spin its own idea of Miss Lizzie and how she became the most infamous madam of Guthrie. Thus this story, and others to follow.

Many residents and business owners of Guthrie contributed information and/or gave permission to fictionalize their businesses: Jane, Claude and Randy Thomas of the Harrison House; Lloyd C. Lentz III whose book *Guthrie, A History of the Capital City, 1889-1910* provided much-needed information and pictures; Craig and Judy Randle of the Blue Bell Saloon; the employees of the Logan County Court House; the staff at The Territorial Museum; Shirley and Bob Powell; the staff of the Scottish Rite Masonic Temple. The mistakes, of course, are all mine! I'm a fiction writer, not a historian, and I took liberty with the original building dates and origins of some of the businesses in order for my story to happen in the way I saw it.

There is a note in the newsletter published by the owners of Miss Lizzie's Bordello. It reads, "Our hope is the same as the girls of the old house, that all our customers leave satisfied." My wish for my readers is the same…that when you turn the last page of this book, you, too, are satisfied with the tale and the romance as I have chosen to spin it.

Enjoy!

Peggy Moreland

Prologue

Guthrie, Oklahoma—1890

On days like today, I yearn for home. With the wind coloring the sky red with dust, the air so thick a person can barely breathe, I long for the ocean and its stretch of white beaches, its crisp, clean, salty breeze. I think, too, of my family, my life in Boston...but the memories do nothing but sadden me and remind me that I can never return. The decision to leave was mine, knowing when I did, my family would never permit me to come home.

The sacrifices made in coming here were great. First my family, my baby, and lastly my heart. Some will say my father was right, that I should have listened to him and stayed away from Ethan. Others who knew Ethan might understand the blindness of my adoration. At any rate, this is my home now, whether by chance or by choice.

To brighten my spirits, I have only to look out my window. The sights and sounds on the street below console me, for they are those of progress, of challenges met but not yet attained. This is a wild territory, as yet unsettled, plagued by problems of bureaucracy and greed. But there is hope here, promises for a future.

Though only recently arrived, I feel very much a part of this community of newcomers. Their enthusiasm fills me with excitement and the desire to be a participant in the settling of this new land. For me it is an opportunity to begin again. A new life, without regret for that which is gone, but with a hand outstretched to grasp at what the future might hold for me....

One

So this is Guthrie, Oklahoma. Callie wrinkled her nose as she drove down Division Street at a slow crawl. Retail shops and offices fronted both sides of the street, mostly contained in one- and two-story buildings, their architecture dating back to the late 1800s and early 1900s. A man lazily whisked a broom across the sidewalk fronting his business, stirring fall leaves and sending them tumbling to the curb.

Wanting to enjoy the full benefit of what remained of the fall day and take in the sights that lay just up ahead and around the corner, Callie whipped into an empty space at the curb and lowered the convertible top of her Jaguar. As she climbed up on the bumper and stretched across the rear of the car to snap the canvas boot in place, an eighteen-wheeler roared by so close, the wind it stirred sucked at her, making her cling to the canvas to maintain her balance. A ribald proposition from the cab of the truck and three short blasts from the truck's air horn let Callie know, in no uncertain terms, what the truck driver thought of the view of her backside.

Frowning, she dropped to the roadside and tugged her leather jacket back over her hips. "Men," she grumbled under her breath. "Their brains are all located just south of their belt buckles."

With an exasperated huff of breath, she climbed back into her car and gunned the engine, kicking up puffs of dried leaves from the road's shoulder as she swerved back onto the street.

Two blocks farther and a street sign for Harrison Avenue had her turning left. Callie did a neat—although illegal—U-turn in the middle of the intersection of Harrison and First streets and parked alongside the curb.

She looked around, frowning. She didn't know what she'd expected to find when she reached her destination, but this hick town certainly wasn't it. More accustomed to the zip and zoom of expressway traffic and Dallas's towering skyline, the town of Guthrie seemed to Callie like a ghost town in comparison.

Stepping from the car, she pulled her hair back from her face, craned her head back and just looked. Three stories of Victorian brown brick marked the Harrison House, her home for the next few weeks. Across First Street, a sign outside the Victor Building boasted antiques, shops and the chamber of commerce office. With dusk quickly settling, the businesses as well as the street looked all but abandoned.

A bark and a scuffling noise sounded behind her and Callie turned, but not in time. Before she had a chance to prepare herself, a huge beast of a dog leapt at her. Planting his paws on her shoulders, the animal knocked her flat over the hood of the car, pinning her between the car's still-warm metal hood and a hundred pounds of muscled fur.

From her position beneath the animal, all Callie could see were black eyes and saliva-dripping fangs. A scream built in her throat, then stuck there as the dog lowered his gaping jaws closer to her face. Squeezing her eyes shut, she buried her fingers in the animal's thick coat, locked her elbows and shoved for all she was worth.

"Baby, heel!"

In response to the shouted command, the dog barked. The sound vibrated from his paws through Callie's body and ripped the air so close to her ear it nearly deafened her. Her eyes still squeezed shut, she continued to struggle beneath the stifling weight, waiting for the dog to sink his fangs into her cheek, or worse, her neck.

As suddenly as it appeared, the weight of the animal disappeared. Her eyes still closed, Callie let her arms fall weakly to her breasts. She lay there, her chest heaving with each indrawn breath.

"Baby, is that any way to greet a newcomer?" she heard a deep, male voice ask. "I've got him now," the man said, sounding nearer. "Do you need help getting up?"

His voice was as close as the dog's breath had been only moments before, and it blew warm against her cheek, bringing with it the scents of tobacco and peppermint. Callie opened one eye to find the man's face only inches above her own. Coal black hair worn long in the back brushed his collar, and a black Stetson shadowed his face. He poked a finger at the brim, levering the hat farther back on his head. A half grin tweaked one side of his mouth and his brown eyes danced with laughter.

If anything humorous had occurred thus far, Callie hadn't seen it! She glared at him through the slit of one eye, then lifted her head a notch and opened both to assure herself he did, in fact, have the animal under control. Struggling to her elbows, she planted a palm at the man's chest and shoved. "No, I don't need help," she stated indignantly as she clamored to her feet.

"Baby didn't mean any harm," he offered by way of an apology as he stepped aside, avoiding an elbow rammed a little too close to his midriff. "That's his way of saying welcome."

"Baby?" Callie paused in the act of straightening her clothes to look down her nose at the dog, wondering how anything so vicious could earn such an innocent name. "I'd hate to see what happens when you sic him on someone," she said dryly.

"Don't usually have the need."

Rubbing at a shoulder that was already beginning to ache, Callie shifted her gaze from the dog to the man, a frown building around her mouth and eyes as she took her first good look at him. He looked like a gunslinger straight off a Western movie set. A black duster draped him from shoulder to mid-calf, below that nothing but a glimpse of jeans and a scuffed pair of boots. The wind caught the hem of his duster and fanned it out, revealing a Western shirt of vibrant reds and blues. Instead of the gun and holster she had expected, a black tooled leather belt banded the waist of his jeans, clasped navel-high by a silver belt buckle the size of a lady's oval hand mirror.

He turned his back on Callie and braced wide, tanned hands on the side of her car, taking in the leather bucket seats and a dashboard with enough controls to confuse a fighter pilot. "You're not from around here."

A statement, not a question, yet Callie felt obligated to answer. "No, I'm from Dallas."

"Nice car," he said as he leaned over to peer into the back seat where her purse, overnight bag and several cameras were stashed.

"Thanks," she murmured grudgingly as she edged closer, not sure whether she should trust the guy or not.

He picked up a Nikon, snapped off the lens cover and put his eye behind the viewfinder. "You a photographer?" he asked as he focused in on Callie.

"Don't—" The shutter clicked and she groaned, dropping the hand she'd raised to stop him.

He lowered the camera. "Don't, what?"

She snatched the Nikon from him. "Mess with my camera," she muttered through tight lips. The pinging sound of water hitting metal had her slowly turning. Baby stood by the front left tire, his leg hiked, relieving himself on her chrome hubcap. Incensed by the audacity of both the dog and his owner, she snapped the lens cover back in place. "Don't they have leash laws in this town?"

When he didn't answer, she whipped her head around to glare at him. The lethal look in his eyes made her take a wary step backward. He held her gaze a good ten seconds that had Callie all but squirming before he settled a hand atop the dog's head and scratched an ear. "Don't need one," he said in a lazy drawl. "The dogs in this town, as well as the residents, are friendly. It's the visitors we have to keep an eye on." He turned on his heel. "Come on, Baby," he called as he strode away.

The black Labrador retriever hesitated, looked at Callie, barked, then finally loped off to follow his owner. Callie watched them both, her chest swelling in anger.

"Well, I never!" With a frustrated huff of breath, she jerked her overnight bag and purse from the back seat and headed across the street to the Harrison House.

"I've been propositioned by a truck driver, mauled by a beast I swear is half wolf and half dog, and put down by a local yokel. Prudy, the nicest thing I can say about the town so far is that it's quaint." Callie tucked the phone receiver between her shoulder and ear and stretched the phone cord as far as it would allow as she ran a hand along the carved front of an antique armoire in her hotel room, one more of the "quaint" features the town boasted.

"If you wanted to be propositioned, all you had to do was stand down on Harry Hines Boulevard with the rest of the hookers, and with the right command from John, Yogi would've taken a chunk out of your leg. 'Quaint' you can find within an hour's drive of downtown Dallas.''

Though the reply was almost acid in delivery, Callie heard the concern beneath. After sharing studio space with Prudy for seven years, the two were more like sisters than business associates, and she'd learned that her friend hid her emotions behind a caustic tongue. "You miss me."

"Hardly. Without your constant distraction, the studio is relatively quiet. I've actually put in a full day at my potter's wheel and put shape to three really unique pieces."

"Ouch! My ego is taking a beating."

"If I thought for one second I could damage your ego, I'd worry." A deep sigh crossed the phone wires, then, "Callie, come home."

"Prudy, I didn't *move* to Guthrie. I'm merely here on vacation."

"A vacation is the Bahamas or Las Vegas or Vale. Guthrie is a hole-in-the-wall and a wild-goose chase you're using as an excuse to escape—"

"Prudy..." Callie warned.

"Well, it's true. Okay, so we all suffer a creative lag now and again, and considering the pressure Stephen's put you under— Oh, I almost forgot. He called."

Callie plopped down on the bed, her shoulders sagging. "Oh, no. You didn't tell him where I was staying, did you?"

"No. But your mother called, too."

"What did *she* want?"

"She wanted me to use my extraordinary persuasive powers to knock some sense into your head."

Callie fell back across the bed, slinging her forearm across her eyes. And to think she'd thought she could escape a confrontation by leaving Stephen and her parents notes and high-tailing it to Oklahoma at her great-grandfather's request before either had time to respond. What a joke! "Well, go ahead. Give it your best shot," she said in a weary voice.

"I'll tell you the same as I told your mother. I don't interfere in other people's lives."

Though she felt more like curling up in a ball and having a good cry, Callie chuckled at the outrageous lie. "That'll be the day."

"It's true! And besides," Prudy added, with an offended sniff, "if I were going to interfere, I'd have stopped you from running away before you even left."

Callie sat bolt upright on the bed. "Prudy! I have not run away. I'm simply fulfilling a request Papa made of me."

"Oh, yes, Papa. The man is one hundred and four years old and about three bricks short of a load. For heaven's sake, Callie. Half the time he doesn't even know who you are. How can you possibly think he could remember enough about your family's history for you to run off on some half-cocked errand to locate his mother's grave for him?"

"Because I love him and because he asked me to and because I needed a vacation. Satisfied?"

"No." Silence followed, then more reluctantly, "Just be careful and hurry home. I do miss you. Sort of."

Anxious to escape her room before her mother or Stephen located her, Callie headed for the lobby. Behind the front desk, a man sat with his head bent, his back to her and seemingly oblivious to her presence as he scribbled entries into a ledger sprawled across a rolltop desk.

An old display case, the bubbles and waves in its glass a testament to its age, separated her from the clerk's desk. The jewelry and trinkets filling it caught her eye, and she stopped to admire then. Colorful stones ensconced in various settings of silver, gold and platinum blinked up at her.

"Would you like to have a closer look?"

Startled, Callie glanced up to find the man still had his back to her. "No, just browsing."

"Here on vacation?"

A particularly interesting cluster of stones on a brooch caught her eye, and she replied offhandedly, "That and a quest."

"Yours wouldn't be the first." Tucking the pen in the valley created by the ledger's swelled pages, he spun his chair around to smile at her. "And what quest would you be on?"

Tufts of white hair puffed over the man's ears and a pair of reading glasses perched precariously on the end of his nose. He looked like an absentminded professor, but it was the openness of his smile that made Callie forget the brooch. After her encounter with the gunslinger on the street earlier, she'd been half-afraid the entire population of Guthrie shared his personality.

Thankful to discover that at least one person didn't, she propped her elbows on the top of the glass and smiled back. "My great-grandfather's to be honest. He asked me to track down some of his family who lived here during the late eighteen hundreds, but the only information I have is the woman's maiden name. I've never done anything like this before. Any suggestions on where I might start?"

"The courthouse, the State Capital Publishing Museum, the Oklahoma Territorial Museum, the historical society, the police records, the—"

"Whoa!" Callie laughed as she straightened to dig a scrap of paper and a pen from her purse. She scribbled the information quickly, then glanced up. "Where else?"

Springs creaked as the man reared back in the chair and folded his arms across his ample middle. "That would depend on what information you have to work with."

Callie shrugged, embarrassed that she had so little to go on. "A name, an approximate time she moved here...that's about it."

He puckered his lips thoughtfully. "All those places I mentioned will be helpful, but if you want to know more, Judd Barker down at the Blue Bell Saloon might be able to help you. He knows everything worth knowing about Guthrie."

Callie tucked the slip of paper into her jacket pocket. Knowing that all the places he'd mentioned would be closed by now, she settled on the suggestion of talking to Judd Barker. "And where do I find the Blue Bell Saloon?"

"One block west on the corner. Can't miss it. Just tell Judd, Frank sent you."

"Thanks." Callie pushed out the door, quickly folding the plackets of her jacket tighter around her as a blast of wind hit her full force. With a shiver she tucked her hands beneath her armpits and headed west in the direction the hotel clerk had suggested. The street both behind and beyond her was abandoned. Lights shone from a few businesses that were still open, but the only sounds in the night came from the click of her bootheels against the brick sidewalk that stretched in front of her and the whine of the wind as it whistled its way into the buildings' nooks and crannies.

Streetlamps cast a golden glow, lighting her way while turning the bricks beneath her feet a rosy hue. Intent on her mission and with her head bowed against the wind, she passed the Victor Building, crossed a short alley, and then a café without offering any of them a second glance. Her steps slowed, though, as she passed a single, weathered door that looked unused and long-forgotten wedged in the wall of brick.

Faint strains of music drifted through the night air, but it was the sound of a woman's laugh that made Callie stop and listen. She glanced at the locked door then inched closer to peer through its dusty glass. Though dark inside, with the aid of the streetlamp behind her she made out a wooden staircase in the narrow hallway beyond, its painted steps worn with time and hollowed with the scrape of feet traveling upwards to a second floor. The building appeared empty, yet Callie was sure the music and laughter she'd heard had come from within.

Using the heel of her fist, she rubbed a clean spot on the dusty glass, then looked again. Shadows danced on the landing above, their forms surreal, ghostlike. A woman's laugh came low and lusty, and Callie could have sworn she heard the woman's invitation to, "Come on up and join us."

Stepping back from the door, she placed a hand over a heart that was thudding a little faster than a moment before. "You're losing it, Callie," she warned beneath her breath. Turning on her heel, she all but ran the remaining distance to the Blue Bell Saloon.

Set in the corner of the building, the bar's door offered welcoming light and the comforting sound of conversation and laughter. Fighting the wind, she wrestled open the door and slipped inside.

While she took a moment to catch her breath, she glanced around. A long bar stretched on her left, behind it a mirror spanned its length. Polished brass gleamed from the footrails of the stools pushed up to the antique bar. On her right, tables covered with linen cloths were arranged in cozy groups for the diners enjoying an evening meal.

She took a step inside, intent on reaching the bar and ordering a hot cup of coffee laced with whiskey to calm her nerves before seeking out Judd Barker. A low growl stopped her—one that sounded frighteningly familiar. Steeling herself, she slowly turned and saw Baby standing between her and the door she'd just entered.

His hair bristled around the collar at his neck and down his spine, and his teeth were bared. Had he followed her in? She stole a glance at the door, expecting it to open and his owner to appear, but there wasn't a sign of the man through the glass. She thought about screaming, but feared that would only upset the dog further. Surely someone in the bar would see the dog and come to her rescue. Keeping her eye on him, she slowly began to back away. "It's okay, Baby," she soothed in a voice pitched low to hide her fear. "I'm not going to hurt you."

Her back hit a wall of flesh and she stopped, her eyes widening in surprise. Not wanting to make any sudden movements, she whispered, "Quick! Get the owner or the manager. This dog followed me in here."

"He didn't follow you, he was here first."

At the sound of the familiar male voice, Callie whirled. "You," she whispered accusingly when her gaze met the brown eyes of Baby's owner.

He spread his arms wide. "None other."

She threw a glance back at the dog to make sure he hadn't snuck up behind her before she turned to glare at the man again. "Isn't there a law against having dogs in bars?"

He shrugged. "Probably. Nobody complains, though. Baby's sort of the mascot of the place."

"Well, *I'm* complaining," she said, stabbing her thumb at her chest for emphasis. She pushed past the irritating man and made for the bar. Angling a hip to slide onto a stool, she folded her hands on the bar and managed a smile for the bartender. "Are you the owner, sir?" she asked politely.

He glanced over her shoulder at the man behind her, then looked down again, hiding a smile. "No, ma'am. I just work here."

"Well, my name is Callie Benson. I'm a visitor in Guthrie, but I've already had one run-in with that dog this afternoon and don't relish another one. Would you mind asking this man to remove the animal, please?"

"I—" The bartender shifted his gaze from hers to a spot above and behind her. Slowly, he shook his head as he returned his gaze to her. "No, ma'am. I'm sorry, but I can't."

Imperiously Callie straightened, adding a good two inches to her height. "Then I would like to speak to the owner, please. Is he here?"

"Yes, ma'am." The bartender picked up a towel, trying real hard not to laugh and said in an overly loud voice,

"Judd, this woman here wants to talk to you. Says she wants you to kick out Baby."

If the bartender had lifted a pistol and squeezed off a shot, he couldn't have stopped the conversation in the room any quicker. In horror Callie watched the mirrored reflection of the room's interior as every occupant turned his head to stare at her.

"Really?"

Callie shifted her gaze on the mirror to focus on the speaker of the single word, the man behind her—Baby's owner. She watched as he moseyed up to the bar beside her.

Nausea quickly replaced horror.

"You're the owner?" she whispered weakly.

"Yep."

She swallowed hard. "Judd Barker?"

"One and the same."

"Oh, God." She dropped her elbows to the bar and her face to her open palms.

"Baby, heel."

Callie heard the pad of Baby's paws and the occasional click of a claw hitting the wooden floor as the dog made his way across the room. Embarrassment kept her eyes hidden beneath her hands.

"Now, Baby," she heard Judd say, "this lady here seems to be holding a grudge against you for the way you greeted her earlier today, and she doesn't think you ought to be in the Blue Bell. My pappy taught me long ago that the customer's always right, but heck, Baby, I sorta' hate to put you out on a night as cold as this one. Can you think of a solution to this problem?"

Callie split her fingers a crack, just enough so she could peek down at the dog. He sat on his haunches not a foot away, his eyes as soulful as a cocker spaniel's and looking for all the world like a repentant child being lectured by his father. She closed her eyes against the sight of him, refusing to soften to the beast who had twice that day scared the living daylights out of her.

The next thing she knew, Baby's front paws were planted on her right thigh and his tongue, as coarse and abrasive as the pumice stone she kept on the side of her sink at the studio, was licking at her pressed fingers.

Steeling herself against the warmth flooding her heart, she knotted her hands on top of the bar, but continued to ignore him.... That is, she did so until she felt the damp, velvety texture of his snout as he nuzzled her cheek and heard the most pitiful whimper rumble low in his chest. Then she crumbled.

"Oh, good heavens," she said, trying to hide the effect he had on her with irritation. He lifted his head and barked twice in rapid succession, then looked at her, panting happily, his tongue lolling, dripping saliva on the leg of her jeans.

Laughing, Callie cuffed him behind his ears and as a reward earned a full lick on the cheek. She looked up at Judd, her eyes dancing. "How do you call off this beast?"

"Baby, sit." Immediately the black Labrador dropped to his haunches beside Callie's barstool, but continued to stare at her with those huge black eyes. She looked right back, but with humor this time, not irritation or fright. Stealing a pretzel from the bowl on the bar, she held one out to him. He nabbed it, then lay down at her feet and happily crunched away.

"Does this mean he can stay?"

Callie turned her head to look at Judd. "Do I have a choice?" She opened a palm and gestured toward the customers in the bar who had gone back to their own private conversations. "Between them and Fido here, I think if push came to shove, *I'd* be the one cast out on the street, not him." She looked down at the dog again and snorted. His paws were as large as her opened hand. "How in the world did a beast like that earn the name Baby?"

Judd sidled up to the bar and lowered a hip to the barstool beside her, his knee brushing her thigh. Heat radiated from his leg to hers. Callie felt it, but didn't draw away. Neither did Judd, although she knew by the slight narrowing of his eyes that he was as aware as she of the contact. She arched one brow slightly as she listened to his explanation.

"He wasn't always this big. Believe it or not, when I first got him, I could hold him in the palm of my hand. He was the runt of a litter of fifteen and about as poor as they come. Why, you could pluck the chords of a song on his rib cage, he was so skinny."

Callie couldn't help but laugh.

"My goodness, Baby," he said in mock surprise. "The lady can smile."

Immediately, her lips puckered into a frown. "Don't push your luck. I still may press charges for assault with intent to kill."

"Baby? Kill? He wouldn't hurt a fly. That's just how he greets people."

Callie looked down at the dog at the same moment Baby looked up. His appearance alone was enough to intimidate a person. Wide, square forehead set off by two pricked ears, shoulders as broad as any professional linebacker and paws as wide as her outspread hand. But his eyes... Once she looked into them, really looked, she knew the dog was a pussycat. His eyes were pure black, but soft and totally endearing. As she looked into them now, she couldn't believe she'd been afraid of this animal.

"Yeah, well..." she said in embarrassment. "He looks innocent enough now, but that growl." She suppressed a shudder, remembering, then cocked her head to look at Judd. "If he's so safe, why did he growl at me like that?"

"He's protective."

"Of what?"

"Not what, whom." He bent to scratch Baby behind the ears. "He thought you might pose a threat to me."

"Me?"

"Yeah." He straightened, and Callie saw a half grin tug at one corner of his mouth. She couldn't help thinking how similar the pet and his owner were. Like his dog, Judd Barker looked meaner than sin. A gunslinger, she remembered thinking when she'd first seen him earlier that evening. And that's exactly what he'd looked like. Tall and lanky, the lines of his face hard and unforgiving.

But now, without the sinister black duster and Stetson, and with that grin softening the hard lines of his face, he looked almost friendly. She was sure he'd deny the comparison, but beneath that rough exterior she would swear lay a heart as soft as Baby's.

"You raised your voice this afternoon, and Baby takes offense at anybody who yells at me. So when you came in the door a minute ago, Baby was just warning you to keep your distance."

"Well, for heaven's sake," she said in exasperation.

"No, for mine." He chuckled and signaled the bartender. "What can I get you to drink?"

"Something warm and strong."

He eyed her a moment, then told the man behind the bar, "A Jersey Mint for the lady and a beer for me." He hooked the heels of his boots over the barstool's brass rail and spun toward her. The graze of starched jeans against her leg was like bumping up against a live electrical wire. The jolt brought every nerve ending in her body humming to life.

"Now tell me," he said, turning his elbows out and splaying his hands on his knees. "What's a beautiful lady like you doing in a place like this?"

The line was old, but delivered with such a smoothness, Callie had to fight back a laugh. That he was a flirt was obvious, but she could give as good as she got. "Looking for you," she said demurely.

The muscles in his neck immediately tensed. "Me?"

"Yes," she replied, chuckling at his raised brow. She extended her hand. "I'm Callie Benson." His fingers closed firmly around hers. Instead of shaking as she'd intended, he merely held her hand in his while he studied her through narrowed eyes.

"And what would a pretty girl like you want with an old cowboy like me?"

The ball of his thumb moved in a slow, seductive arc across her knuckles while he asked the question, and Callie had to swallow twice before she could form an answer. "The hotel clerk at the Harrison House said you might be able to help me."

"In what way?"

The bartender appeared and shoved a steaming mug topped with whipped cream and shaved chocolate in front of her. Thankful for the excuse to remove her hand from the heat of Judd's, Callie accepted the mug with a grateful smile. She took a tentative sip, and her eyes widened in surprise. "This is delicious. What is it?"

"A Jersey Mint. Hot chocolate with a shot of peppermint schnapps and wallop of whipped cream on top. Thought you might enjoy the taste."

"It's wonderful!" She sipped again, letting the warmth of the drink penetrate while savoring the minty, chocolaty flavor. "Anyway," she said as she licked at her upper lip to capture the smudge of whipped cream that stuck there, "I'm trying to locate information about my great-grandfather's mother, and the clerk said you might be able to help me. I have her name and the approximate date of her arrival in Guthrie." She wrinkled her nose. "Unfortunately, that's all I've got."

"People have had less and found what they needed. What's the woman's name?"

"Mary Elizabeth Sawyer."

The beer halfway to his mouth, Judd froze, his hand halting just short of his lips. Slowly, he lowered his gaze to hers and the mug to his thigh. "Mary Elizabeth Sawyer?"

"Yes."

"And you say she's your great-grandfather's mother?"

"Yes. Have you heard of her?"

Judd stared at her, his eyes darkening and narrowing with what Callie could only describe as suspicion. After a moment, he dropped his gaze to the frosted mug of beer, then lifted the glass and drained it. As he lowered the mug, he swiped the back of his hand across his mouth. Pressing his fists to his knees, he rose. "Maybe. I'll let you know." He shoved the empty glass across the bar. "Hank," he called to the bartender. "The lady's drink is on the house." He slapped a hand to his jeans. "Come on, Baby."

Two

Judd stood in the narrow alleyway, one shoulder propped against the rough brick wall and a hand stuffed deep in the pocket of his jeans. A ribbon of smoke curled lazily upward from the cigarette dangling from his lips. Baby lay at his feet, his head resting between his front paws. Judd's gaze was pitched high on the brick wall opposite him to a square of newer brick he could just make out in the dim light.

At one time a catwalk had crossed from the building opposite his into the second story of the building his bar was housed in. At some point in time, someone had seen fit to remove the catwalk and had bricked up the openings in both buildings.

But the memory of its purpose remained.

Sighing, Judd pulled the cigarette from his mouth and flicked it away. He hunkered down beside Baby and dropped a hand to scratch absently at the dog's head. As was his habit, the animal rolled to his back, exposing his belly. Chuckling, Judd scratched him there, as well. "You big lug," he said in gentle reproach. He sighed again as he lifted his gaze back to the wall.

If the woman had asked about anything or anyone else, he would have given her what information he could and sent her on her way without a second thought. But the lady had made a mistake. A big one. Mary Elizabeth Sawyer—the woman she claimed was her great-grandfather's mother— had never had any children. At least none who had lived.

All of which led Judd to wonder who Callie Benson really was, and what she wanted. The options were limited, for what would bring anyone to Guthrie, Oklahoma? The town was small, businesses few. Guthrie's only draws were the Lazy E Rodeo Arena and the bed-and-breakfast inns that served the tourists who came to enjoy a bit of history.

She sure as hell wasn't a cowboy. A tourist, then? He shook his head at the thought. Granted she had a car full of cameras, but they weren't the standard equipment a tourist would carry. More like a professional photographer's gear. To his way of thinking, that only left one purpose for her visit. She'd come to dig up more dirt on Judd Barker. As if enough dirt hadn't been heaped on his name already.

He heaved another sigh. "So what are we going to do, Baby? Call her hand?"

In response, the dog whined low in his throat. The sound vibrated through Judd's fingertips and drew a rueful smile. Baby was his oldest friend, and at times in his life, his only friend.

Baby's ears perked, and he sat up and growled. Judd placed a restraining hand on the dog's head to quiet him, and listened. He heard the faint click of footsteps on the brick sidewalk on the street beyond and took a step back to fade deeper into the alley's shadows. Moments later he watched as Callie passed by the alley's opening, her head bent against the wind, her shoulders hunched against the cold.

She didn't look like a reporter, at least not the sleazy variety who'd hounded him in the past. She looked like money, old money, the kind who dressed as they pleased and thumbed their noses at fashion. The leather jacket she wore was soft and supple with age. She wore it with a disregard for its value that only the privileged could pull off. Her jeans were even older than her jacket and threadbare in places that made a man look twice.

And her car. Jesus. The sticker price on it alone was higher than that on most of the houses in Guthrie.

As he watched her disappear from sight, the rounded cheeks of her butt playing a game of "now you see me, now you don't" beneath the hem of her jacket, he curled his fingers in Baby's fur. That he was attracted to her didn't surprise him. Last time he checked, he wasn't blind or dead—yet. And Callie Benson was a beautiful woman. Hers was a God-given beauty, nothing fake or implanted or modified about her. And, with his experience, Judd should know.

He had a reputation as a lady's man, and he couldn't deny the tag. The guys in the band and in his road crew used to have an ongoing bet to see how long it took Judd to get laid once he hit a new town. To him it wasn't a competition, only the simple pleasure of a pretty woman and—if she was willing—good sex. He knew no other kind.

Yep, in the past a woman out on the prowl, looking for a good time, would've found it with Judd Barker.

But not anymore. He'd learned to curb his appetite for the taste and feel of a pretty woman.

"Liar," he muttered under his breath. He slapped a hand against his leg and headed for the rear door that led to his bar with Baby padding along at his heels.

Callie burst through the door of the hotel, her arms wrapped tight around her. Frank turned and looked up at her over the top of his glasses. "Cold out?"

"Freezing!"

He chuckled and gave his chair a push, spinning around to face her. "It's the wind. Cuts right through a person."

"That's for sure." She shivered and dropped her arms to shake them in an attempt to get her blood flowing warm again.

"Did you find Judd?"

She stopped flapping long enough to frown. "Yeah, I found him, all right." She crossed to the front desk and propped her elbows on its top, puckering her lips into a pout. "What is it with that man? Does he eat nails for breakfast, or what?"

"Judd?" Frank chuckled and reared back in his chair, lacing his hands behind his head. "Nah, he just doesn't take to strangers." He leaned forward to scrape some papers from his desk. "Had a call or two while you were out." He stretched to pass the messages to Callie.

"Thanks, Frank." Frowning, she stuffed the papers into her pocket without looking at them. The burden of them made her shoulders sag, but she forced a smile. "Well, I guess I'll call it a night. See you in the morning."

"Sure thing. We start serving breakfast at eight."

Once in the privacy of her room, Callie shrugged out of her jacket, then held it by its sleeve while she dug in the pocket for the messages Frank had given her. She tossed the jacket to the bed as she opened the first.

Call Stephen—214-555-5622.

She sank down on the bed and unfolded the second message.

Call Stephen. Urgent—214-555-5622.

She fell back, groaning, her hand moving to shove her hair from her eyes. In the note she'd left him, she had asked for space, time. Obviously, Stephen wasn't going to honor either request.

A knock at the door had her jackknifing to a sitting position. Frowning, she scooted off the bed and crossed to the door. Standing on tiptoe, she peered through the peephole. All she could see was unrelieved black, which in itself was enough to identify her visitor. The outline of a Stetson pulled low on the man's forehead only served to confirm who stood outside.

Grimacing, she flung open the door. "A little late for a social call, don't you think?"

He planted a hand on either side of the frame and leaned toward her, his gaze boring deep into hers. "Who are you?"

A frown puckered between her brows at his threatening look, and she took a cautious step back. "Callie Benson."

"So you said." He stepped inside, blocking any chance of her slamming the door in his face. "But what I want to know is *what* you are. Why you're here."

Unconsciously, she lifted a hand to her throat, wondering if Frank would hear if she screamed loud enough. "I told you, to find information on my great-grandfather's mother."

His hand arced out, fanning the air narrow inches from her nose. "Cut the bull. Mary Elizabeth Sawyer never had any children."

Callie fell back a step. "I beg your pardon?"

"She never had children. None that lived, anyway."

"She most certainly did!" She whirled to grab her purse. "I have the papers right here to prove it." She dug in the depths of her feed-bag style purse, pulled out yellowed documents and thrust them under his nose. "See for yourself. William Leighton Sawyer, born June 14, 1890, Oklahoma Territory. Son of Mary Elizabeth Sawyer."

Judd looked at the paper, then shoved her hand aside. "There's a tombstone out in Summit View Cemetery that carries the same information."

Callie's mouth dropped open, then clamped shut with an indignant click of teeth. "I'll have you know my great-grandfather is William Leighton Sawyer, and he might be old, but he's very much alive."

"You're a reporter, aren't you?"

"A reporter!" she repeated, her voice rising in anger and frustration. "No, I'm not a reporter. I'm a—" She threw up her hands, unable to believe she was even having this conversation. "I don't owe you any explanations. Now get out of my room, or I'll call Frank and have you thrown out."

When he didn't move, she reached for the phone. He caught her arm at the wrist and pulled it to his thigh, dragging her to stand nose-to-nose with him. "You came to find me, didn't you?"

Callie's chest swelled in anger. "What are you? Some kind of egomaniac? I don't know you, and furthermore, don't care to know you. Now, if you don't mind," she said through clenched teeth as she tried to wrench free of him. "Get your hands off me."

Instead of releasing her, he tightened his fingers on her wrist, making her wince. "Look me in the eye and tell me you've never heard of Judd Barker."

She lifted her gaze to his and glared right back at the cold, hate-filled eyes pinned on her. "No, I've never heard of—" She stiffened as the name clicked a hidden memory, one of headlines with the name in bold, dark type. Judd Barker—Country Western's Favorite Son Gone Bad.

She wasn't a fan of country music, but like every other person who'd ever stood in a grocery checkout line, she'd read the headlines on the tabloids racked there. She would have dismissed them for the sensationalistic trash they were, except she'd also seen the cover of "People Weekly" magazine and read the story within. Judd Barker Charged With Rape Of Fan.

He watched her eyes darken in fear and felt the kick of it in her pulse through his fingertips. Her reaction both sickened and angered him. "So you have heard of me."

"Ye-yes," she stammered.

"And you came to see for yourself what kind of man would rape a defenseless woman and maybe get a front-page story for your trouble? Well, take a good look, sweetheart. This may be the only chance you get."

Her head wagged back and forth in mute denial before she found her voice. "No. No, I told you. I didn't come here to find you. I came to trace my great-grandfather's mother."

He twisted her hand behind his waist, dragging her body flush against his. He fisted his other hand in her hair, yanking her head back, forcing her face up to his. "Liar."

Unwanted tears budded in her eyes. Her neck ached with the strain of looking up at him, but she was no match for his strength. Refusing to show her fear, she met his gaze squarely. "I'm not lying. And if you do not remove your hands from me by the time I count to three, I'm going to scream bloody hell and have everyone in the hotel in this room." She narrowed her eyes, levering a note of threat into her voice as she added, "With one charge of rape of against you, you might have a hard time explaining your presence in my room. One. Two. Thr—"

His face came down, his lips crushing against hers, absorbing the scream that built in her throat. Her heart slammed against her chest at the first shocking contact. He's going to rape me, she thought incredulously as she instinctively strained against the hand that held her face to his. Or kill me, she thought on a shudder. And she didn't know which would be worse.

With every ounce of strength within her, she fought him, twisting her wrist within fingers cinched like a steel band, shoving against a chest, iron-hard with padded muscle. Her attempts to escape were futile for his mouth continued to punish her for a wrong she couldn't name.

Her wrist throbbed from the effort, her neck ached from the strain, yet she continued to struggle as his lips persisted in their bruising assault.

Then it changed. Everything. In the span of a heartbeat, his fingers loosened in her hair to cup her nape, his grip on her hand disappeared only to reappear, softer, gentler, at her waist. The lips on hers no longer punished, but teased; his tongue hot and wet, tracing the seam of her lips, skimming down her throat to savor the smooth skin there.

She found the sudden change from abductor to seducer as debilitating as his strength had been only moments ago. She knew that nothing held her to this man any longer, but she couldn't—didn't—pull away.

Instead, she curled her fingers into his shirt and clung. Against the flat of her palm, his heart beat. The back of her hand monitored her own heart's thundered response. Passion, the kind she'd dreamed of but wasn't sure existed, heated the blood coursing through her veins, turning her skin to fire, her sanity to a pile of ash.

He lifted a hand to nudge off his hat. It hit the floor, bounced against her leg then rocked slowly to a stop at her feet. Her fingers climbed up his chest to anchor on his shoulders. Her chest heaved with each intake of breath, her nipples hardening with each scrape of silk against cotton.

Her reaction to him both shocked and repulsed her. This man was a total stranger...a suspected rapist...and yet there was nothing strange about the way she felt in his arms. There was a familiarity in the way they responded to each other, an instantaneous spark of recognition that defied reason.

She dropped her head back on a low moan. "Don't," she whispered.

"Don't, what?" he murmured, his breath heating the soft skin of her throat before he returned his lips to hers. He leveled his hands on her waist, then skimmed slowly upward over her ribs.

"Don't—" She sucked in a ragged breath when his thumbs pushed against the swell of her breasts, sending rivers of sensation flooding through her. "You've got to stop," she cried on a broken sob. "Or else I'll— I'll—"

His body went rigid against hers. "Or else you'll what?" He took a step back, branding her with eyes dark with loathing. "Scream rape?" With his gaze still locked on hers, he bent and scooped his hat from the floor and fitted it over his head. He ran a finger along the brim to pull it low over his eyes.

"It's not rape when a woman's willing," he said, then spun and walked to the door, his black duster swishing against the legs of his starched jeans. He stopped, one hand braced high on the door, then turned to look at her over his shoulder. "And you, sweetheart, were more than willing."

Hours later Callie lay on her back, the sheet and blanket clutched to her chin, her eyes wide, staring at the ceiling overhead. Though the thermostat in the room registered a comfortable seventy-two degrees, shivers shook her body.

He'd been wrong. She hadn't been willing. She'd been desperate, almost crazy with her need for him. If he hadn't stopped when he did, she wasn't at all sure she could have found the strength to end what he had started.

Even now, with regret stinging her eyes and throat, an ache still throbbed between her legs, crying out for a satisfaction she knew she shouldn't want.

A sob rose in her throat, and she caught her lower lip between her teeth, holding it back. She'd always known there was more between a man and a woman than what she'd experienced. More than just a physical joining. There had to be a higher level, an almost spiritual experience that transformed a man and a woman when they touched. She'd never experienced that with Stephen, which explained her hesitancy in agreeing to set a date for their marriage.

But she had felt "that something different" with Judd Barker. God help her, but she'd felt it.

"Prudy, I want you to fax me everything you can find on Judd Barker."

"The country-western singer?"

Callie juggled the phone between her ear and shoulder while she laced up her hiking boots. "Yes."

"For heaven's sake, why?"

She caught the phone in her hand, tightening her fingers on the receiver as she lurched to her feet. "Look, I don't have time to explain right now. I'm on my way to the cemetery to see Papa's grave."

"Papa's! He's not dead! You're supposed to be looking for his mother's grave. Callie, what is going on? Are you all right?"

Callie closed her eyes and pressed a hand to her forehead, not sure that she'd ever be all right again. Not after last night. But she wouldn't trouble Prudy with that now. "Yes," she replied. "I'm fine. I'm just in a hurry. I'll call later and explain."

She hung up before Prudy could demand an immediate explanation. Gathering up her jacket and purse, she headed out the door. She avoided the elevator and took the stairs, shrugging on her jacket as she went, hoping to escape the hotel without seeing anyone. She slipped out the side door and shoved sunglasses onto her nose. Thankfully, the wind was gone, the air crisp and clear, the sun almost blinding it was so bright.

She crossed quickly to her car, unlocked the door and tossed in her purse. Leaning over, she pushed the button to lower the top, then moved to the back of the car to snap the boot in place. A streak of black flashed past her, nearly making her jump out of her skin. She turned to find Baby perched in the back seat.

Glowering at the dog, she marched to the open door. "Out!" she ordered, her index finger pointing in the direction she expected him to take. The black Lab simply looked at her, his tongue lolling, his tail swishing across the leather seat. She planted a knee in the bucket seat, stretched to close a hand around the dog's collar and tugged. Baby braced himself and tugged just as effectively in the opposite direction. After a good two minutes of tug-of-war with the stubborn beast, Callie gave up.

"Fine," she muttered under her breath. "You can ride along, but you better watch your manners," she warned. "And no drooling on the seats," she added as she twisted around and dropped down behind the steering wheel.

Gunning the engine, she peeled away from the curb, sending leaves spinning in whirlwinds behind her rear tires. After giving her sunglasses an impatient shove back on her nose, she dug into her purse for the directions Frank had given her earlier that morning for Summit View Cemetery.

Once she reached the cemetery, she'd prove Judd Barker to be the lying snake that he was, she promised herself as she braked for a red light. Her fingers drummed on the steering wheel in impatience. She'd walk the entire cemetery if necessary, look at every headstone and marker, and when she didn't locate one with William Leighton Sawyer's name on it, then she'd find Judd Barker and—

She glanced at her reflection in the rearview mirror. And what? she asked herself. Have him tarred and feathered and run out of town? The image drew a smug smile.

It isn't rape when a woman's willing. And you, sweetheart, were more than willing. A shiver chased down her spine at the memory and her frown disappeared.

She despised him for his cockiness. She despised him more because he'd been right.

A horn blared behind her and a man's voice yelled, "Hey! What shade of green do you want?"

Scowling at the man in the rearview mirror, she shifted into first gear, pressed the accelerator to the floorboard, then tossed back her head and laughed when she saw the look of surprise on his face when she left him in a cloud of dust.

Frank's directions proved easy to follow, and within minutes she drove between the limestone pillars and black wrought-iron gates marking the cemetery's entrance. The cemetery was laid out just as Frank had described. A tree-lined drive led to a center island where the United States flag and that of Oklahoma waved and snapped in the wind. The island served as the hub while narrow paved lanes fed off of it like spokes, dividing the cemetery into neat sections.

Callie parked beneath an elm tree and sagged back in her seat as she looked around, overwhelmed by the number of markers scattered across the hill. "Come on, Baby," she muttered in resignation as she climbed from her car. "We might as well get started."

Baby bounded out of the back seat and trotted along beside her. They walked for over an hour, with Baby occasionally darting away to chase a squirrel up a tree or a rabbit into his burrow. With each passing marker, Callie's original purpose for the trip was forgotten as emotion built, tightening her throat. Infants, young children, young wives. Each marker she read reflected the hard life of the early settlers of Guthrie and the tolls it took. One in particular caught her attention, and she stopped, studying the grave of a mother and infant buried together.

Sighing, she walked on to the next marker. The surname BODEAN topped the double-wide marker and below it the names Jedidiah to the left and Mary Elizabeth to the right.

Mary Elizabeth? She knelt in front of the marker and, using her thumbnail, scraped away the gold-brown moss which had attached itself to the etchings in the granite and noted the dates. The age according to the year of birth would be approximately right for her great-great-grandmother's, but the stone read that the woman had died in 1938. That would have made her sixty-seven years of age when she'd passed away, and Papa's mother had died in childbirth.

Certain that she was wasting her time, she took a pen and paper from her purse and jotted down the dates of the couple's births and deaths in order to check them with the court records later.

With a little less than half the cemetery covered, she pushed to her feet. "Come on, Baby. Let's go." She strode off, but stopped and looked back when she heard Baby whimpering. The dog stood at the edge of the plot, clawing at the ground. Dead grass and dirt flew beneath his front paws.

"Baby! No!" Callie ran to clamp a hand around the dog's collar and haul him back. "You mustn't dig here." Feeling responsible for the dog's desecration of the grave site, Callie dropped to her knees to scrape the dirt back in place. She bit back an oath when her finger rammed something hard. Curious, she smoothed the dirt away and saw the edge of a flat granite stone. Using the palm of her hand she whisked away the dirt and dead grass covering it, then shoved her sunglasses to the top of her head.

William Leighton Sawyer
Infant Son of Mary Elizabeth Sawyer
June 14, 1890

She sat down hard on her heels and dragged her hands to her knees. "No," she murmured, shaking her head in denial. "No, it can't be."

She dug her nails into the fabric at her knees, clinging to reason. William Leighton Sawyer hadn't died at birth. He had lived a very full life, fathering two sons himself while parlaying the Boston Sawyers' wealth to new highs in Texas oil.

He'd outlived both his sons and saw three of his grandchildren—one of which was Callie's mother—start their own families, giving him four great-grandchildren. He had ruled the dynasty he'd created from the eighteenth floor of the office building he owned in downtown Dallas before he'd been forced into retirement at the age of ninety-eight by Callie's father and a handful of greedy relatives who couldn't wait for him to die so they could get their hands on his money.

They'd said he was crazy, although the legal papers they'd drawn against him read mentally incompetent. Callie had never considered him crazy. Eccentric, yes, but who wasn't in their own way?

Throughout her life, she'd heard the stories about Papa. How his mother had run away from home, chasing after some smooth-talking stranger on his way to the Oklahoma Territory to seek his fortune. How the man had gotten her pregnant and abandoned her without marrying her once they'd arrived in the wild territory. And how she'd died giving birth to Papa.

Cousins from Boston who'd come to Texas to visit during the summers would whisper stories of how Papa was considered the renegade in the family, just like his mother. It was that streak of wildness that had carried him to Texas, they'd said, much to the dismay of the grandparents who'd taken him in and raised him as their own. Papa had thumbed his nose at them all and their high-society ways and proceeded to build a fortune that made the Boston Sawyers look like poor white trash in comparison.

Always strong and full of energy, but with the power of his businesses stripped from him, Papa's health had quickly faded and his focus had shifted to his past. His mother had become his obsession. Her life in Oklahoma and his part in her death seemed to haunt him. He wanted to find where she'd been buried and ensure she'd received a proper burial. Although the rest of the family had pooh-poohed his request as just one more outrageous demand from a crazy old man, Callie had agreed to help him.

A tear streaked down her face followed quickly by another, then another, until her shoulders shook with sobs as she stared at the slab of granite. Guilt stabbed at her, for her reasons in agreeing to help Papa weren't purely unselfish. Yes, she loved him and wanted to help him, but she'd also wanted to get out of Dallas, and Papa's request for help had been the excuse she'd needed.

With the deadline quickly approaching for a signed commission sculpture she couldn't seem to create, and Stephen's and her mother's constant pressure for her to set a wedding date, she'd needed to escape it all. In her mind, that put her in the same category as the rest of her family. Selfish, greedy and spineless. She'd thought she could locate the grave, take a picture for Papa and maybe find a few tidbits of information about his mother for him, then spend the rest of her vacation working out her own personal problems.

And now this.

Baby dropped down beside her, nuzzling his snout against her hand. Hardly aware of her movements, she shifted a hand to scratch his ears. He lifted his head and licked at the tears on her cheek, whimpering low in his throat.

"Oh, Baby." Callie threw her arms around the dog's neck and buried her face in his fur. "Now what am I going to do?"

"You can start by letting loose my dog."

Callie opened her eyes to find a pair of scuffed boots planted not a foot from her knee. She raised her gaze, skimming it over jeans and a black duster until her eyes met the accusing ones of Judd Barker.

She immediately turned away, hiding her tears. Heat flooded her face as she remembered all too clearly the way she'd responded to him the night before. "I didn't steal your dog," she mumbled.

"Didn't say you did," Judd replied, although that was exactly the thought that had crossed his mind when Frank had told him he'd seen Callie drive away earlier that morning with Baby riding in the back seat of her car.

Callie dropped her hands from around Baby's neck and swiped at her cheeks. "You insinuated as much. But the truth of the matter is, your dog jumped in the back of my car and wouldn't get out. It was easier to just let him ride along."

Judd hunkered down beside them, placing a hand on Baby's head. "When he sets his mind on something, he's hard to sway."

Callie sniffed and gazed off in the distance, refusing to look at him.

Judd nodded in the direction of the stone. "I see you found what you were looking for."

Without favoring him a glance, Callie replied sharply, "I don't know that I have."

"Seems clear enough to me. There's the stone bearing the name William Leighton Sawyer, infant son of Mary Elizabeth Sawyer. And there—" he said with a nod toward the larger upright stone "—is the grave of Mary Elizabeth Bodean. What more proof do you need?"

She snapped her head around to glare at him. "I don't know for a fact that Mary Elizabeth Sawyer and Mary Elizabeth Bodean were one and the same person."

The streak of tears on her face took Judd by surprise, for he couldn't imagine what the woman would have to cry about. The grave was more than a hundred years old, so she couldn't have any affection for the infant buried there. Which led him to believe that more than likely she was crying because she'd been caught in her lies. Still, the tears moved him. He tucked his duster behind his hip and dug in his back pocket for a handkerchief. He held it out to Callie.

"It's clean," he assured her when she hesitated.

"Thanks," she mumbled grudgingly as she accepted it. She mopped her eyes, then blew her nose.

"Why the tears?"

The question made fresh ones well in her eyes. Grimacing, she balled the handkerchief in her fist. "I'm just tired, is all. I didn't sleep well last night." As soon as the words were out, she regretted them, knowing that with his ego,

Judd would naturally assume thoughts of him were what kept her awake. Biting her lower lip, she glanced away.

Judd hadn't slept well, either, but he wouldn't tell her that. He didn't trust this woman any farther than he could throw her, but he couldn't deny the fact that she had aroused a craving in him that he'd kept under harness for the better part of a year. Just his luck to be tempted by another lying wench.

Because he wasn't willing to confess to his own lack of sleep or the reason for it, he thought it only fair to ease her embarrassment. "Always had trouble sleeping in a strange bed, myself."

If she heard him, she didn't acknowledge it, for she continued to ignore him, staring off in the distance. She looked so pitiful, kneeling there in the dirt, looking so forlorn and lost that Judd was tempted to comfort her. He quickly squelched the urge. He didn't need this headache.

Sighing, he pushed against his knees to stand above her. "Sorry if Baby made a nuisance of himself." He shuffled his feet, not sure what else to say, but feeling something more was needed. "If you want to verify that Mary Elizabeth Sawyer and Mary Elizabeth Bodean are one and the same, you can check the records over at the Logan County Courthouse."

"I intend to."

Her acidic tone made him wish he'd kept the helpful advice to himself. The woman had an attitude and seemed determined to take her hostilities out on him.

"Come on, Baby," he said, slapping a hand to his thigh. "Let's go home." He turned away, vowing that they'd be churning ice cream in hell before he offered any more help to Callie Benson.

Three

"Here it is!" The court clerk spun the heavy ledger toward Callie and pointed to an entry dated August 1, 1891. Callie's heart sank as she read the entry the woman indicated. Throughout the trip from the cemetery to the Logan County Courthouse she'd held on to the thread of hope that Mary Elizabeth Sawyer and Mary Elizabeth Bodean were two different women. But the proof was there before her eyes: "Mary Elizabeth Sawyer and Jedidiah Bodean, wed on August 1, 1891." The words were blurred on the yellowed page, but legible, and they forced her to accept the truth.

Mary Elizabeth Sawyer hadn't died in childbirth as her great-grandfather had been led to believe. She'd married Jedidiah Bodean, and—if the information on the tombstone was accurate—had lived to the ripe old age of sixty-seven.

Then why had Papa, as an infant, been returned to Boston to be raised by his grandparents? she wondered. And why had he been told his mother had died? The answer was obvious and had Callie sinking into a chair, her knees no longer able to support her.

His mother hadn't wanted him. And now it was up to Callie to tell Papa that the mother whose death he'd blamed himself for all these long years hadn't died as a result of his birth. The truth was, she hadn't cared enough about her son to keep him. Anger burned through Callie for the injustice to her great-grandfather.

"Ma'am? Are you all right?"

Callie lifted her head. "Y-y-yes," she stammered as she slowly rose. "I'm fine." She raked her fingers through her hair, but her thoughts weren't as easily gathered as the strands of hair that had fallen across her face. She looked up at the clerk. "I need to find out more about these people. By any chance, have you ever heard of them or a family of that name?"

The woman offered an apologetic smile. "No, I'm sorry. I'm not originally from Guthrie. My husband and I moved here two years ago." Her smile brightened. "But I know someone who might be able to help. No one knows more about Guthrie than—"

Callie feared she knew what was coming, because the description so resembled the one Frank had given the night before. "Judd Barker," she said, finishing the sentence for the clerk, her shoulders sagging.

"Him, too," the woman said, tipping her head in acknowledgement. "But I was going to suggest you talk to Molly Barker, Judd's mother. She used to teach Oklahoma history over at the high school, but she's retired now. Spends most of her time doing volunteer work for the historical society."

Though she wasn't sure she wanted to talk to Judd Barker's mother, or even what she'd ask if she did decide to, Callie dutifully jotted down the location of the historical society headquarters, then gestured toward the ledger.

"Would it be possible for me to get a copy of this document?"

The woman picked up the large volume. "Certainly. It'll only take a minute."

Callie waited, curling her fingers against the chair's back, wishing like hell she'd never heard of Guthrie, Oklahoma. She'd have been a lot better off staying in Dallas, dealing with Stephen face-to-face and leaving Papa's memories of his mother intact.

Callie opened the door of the Harvey Olds House Museum where she'd been told she would locate Mrs. Barker, to find a woman dressed in a period costume standing at the end of a short hall.

"Mrs. Barker?"

The woman turned, pulling off her glasses. "Yes?"

Callie extended her hand. "I'm Callie Benson. A clerk at the courthouse thought you might be able to help me. I'm trying to trace some of my family."

The woman's smile was genuine and warm as she took Callie's hand in greeting. "I'd be happy to assist in any way I can." She waved Callie into the parlor toward an antique settee while she took the rocker opposite it. "Callie Benson," she replied thoughtfully, settling her skirt and petticoats around her. She tapped the earpiece of her glasses against her lower lip as she studied Callie. "Your name is awfully familiar. Were you one of my students?"

Callie smiled patiently. "No, I'm a visitor to Guthrie."

The woman blew out a relieved breath, sending wisps of grey hair that had escaped her bun, flying. "Thank goodness. I didn't think my memory had faded that badly." She put the toe of a high-topped shoe to the floor, settled her hands on the chair's curved arms and gently started the chair rocking. "So, how can I be of assistance?"

"Well, I'm not sure," Callie replied hesitantly. "I'm trying to locate information about Jedidiah and Mary Elizabeth Bodean. Have you heard of them?"

"The Bodeans!" she parroted. "Lands, yes! One of Guthrie's first families. Jedidiah made the run in 1889 and claimed himself some prime real estate in what is now downtown Guthrie. You see, because of the law's governing townships in the new territory, Guthrie at that time was divided into four sections: Capital Hill, West Guthrie, Guthrie Proper and East Guthrie." She batted a hand, chuckling, and sent the chair rocking again. "But you didn't come here for a history lesson, did you, dear?"

"Oh, no, please. It's fascinating."

"Yes, it is. But, then, I love history. But you wanted to know about the Bodeans. Now, what exactly can I tell you about them?"

"Everything. I wasn't even aware Mary Elizabeth had married until I saw the tombstone."

"My, yes, she married. Such a romantic tale. As the story goes, Jedidiah courted Miss Sawyer for over a year before she agreed to marry him. Jedidiah was a bit of a rake. Had his hands in all kinds of businesses, a few of which some of the townspeople didn't approve," she added, arching a knowing brow at Callie. "There was also another complication. You see, Miss Sawyer believed she was in love with someone else, then along came Jedidiah and swept her off her feet." She tipped back her head and laughed merrily. "Although I'm quite sure Jedidiah wouldn't agree with the term 'swept,' being as it took him over a year to convince her to marry him."

"Did they have children?"

"No." She shook her head sadly. "Not together, anyway. Elizabeth had a child before they married, but the child died at birth. Times were hard then. No doctors or hospitals to speak of. Usually women helping women through the births." She knitted her forehead in concern and leaned toward Callie. "Did I say something to upset you, dear?"

Callie scraped the heels of her hands across her cheeks to swipe at the hot tears. She tried to smile, but couldn't. She was too damned mad. "No, it's nothing you said. It's just that Mary Elizabeth Sawyer's son, the one everyone insists died at birth, is my great-grandfather."

Mrs. Barker reared back, her eyes wide. "Great-grandfather?" she repeated.

Callie dug in her purse and pulled out the faded paper on which Papa's birth was recorded. "This is his birth certificate," she said as she passed the paper to Molly. "Contrary to popular belief, William Leighton Sawyer is very much alive and lives in a nursing home in Dallas, Texas."

Molly placed her reading glasses back on her nose and studied the document. "It looks real enough," she murmured.

"I assure you," Callie replied indignantly, "it is."

Molly leaned to pat Callie on the knee. "I'm sorry, dear. I didn't mean to infer that you weren't honest. I just don't know what to make of all of this."

"Nor do I."

Molly passed the document back. "Makes a person wonder if there wasn't foul play of some sort." She sighed. "I guess we'll never know."

"Oh, yes we will."

Molly raised a brow. "But that was over a hundred years ago. How will you ever unravel it all now?"

"I don't know, but I'm not going back to Dallas until I find out the truth."

"That kind of research will take time," Molly warned. "Can you be away from your family and your job that long?"

Stephen came to mind, if only briefly, but Callie quickly discarded the thought. "Family isn't a problem." Her thoughts shifted to the statue she'd been commissioned to sculpt for the new women's wing at a hospital in Houston. The deadline for that silently ticked nearer—yet another point of stress in an already stressful life. "As far as my job goes, I do have a project I'm working on. But I can do that here as easily as at home, although I'll require more space than my room at the Harrison House offers."

"If there is anything I can do to help, dear—"

"Perhaps you can," Callie said, her mind already jumping ahead to everything she'd need to arrange. "I need to lease a place to work. At least for the month. Nothing fancy. Just lots of room and light. Do you know of anything available?"

Molly pursed her lips as she reflected on the question. "I don't know if it would suit your needs, but I own a building just a couple of blocks from the Harrison House. The upstairs is vacant and has been for years." She lifted her wrist to glance at her watch. "I won't be through here until after four o'clock. If you'd like to meet me, I could show you the place. Then you can decide for yourself."

The front door slammed and both women turned to find Judd standing in the entry. "Decide, what?" he asked as he crossed the narrow distance to the parlor.

Callie's stomach muscles tensed at the sight of him while a smile bloomed on Molly's face. "Come and meet Callie Benson. Callie, this is my son, Judd Barker."

Judd stopped beside his mother's chair and frowned at Callie, still feeling the sting of her sharp tongue. "We've met."

"You have?" Molly asked, her gaze shifting from one unsmiling face to another.

"Yeah, at the Blue Bell."

"Did she mention she's a descendant of the Bodeans?"

Judd's lips twisted in derision as he looked down at Callie. "Oh, so now you're claiming kin to the Bodeans, huh?"

Indignant, Callie rose to her feet, stuffing the birth certificate back in her purse. "Not the Bodeans. Mary Elizabeth Sawyer."

Molly flapped a hand. "My fault, dear. This is just all so confusing."

Callie tore her gaze from Judd's to offer Molly a tight smile. "That's quite all right. I'm having a rather difficult time absorbing it all myself."

Judd's snort didn't escape Callie's or his mother's notice.

Callie chose to ignore him and hitched her purse strap higher on her shoulder. "I really should be going. Thank you for visiting with me, Mrs. Barker."

Molly rose as well. "Molly, dear. Call me Molly. Everyone does. And it was my pleasure." She walked with Callie to the door. "Why don't we plan to meet at the Blue Bell Saloon at five this afternoon? That way if I'm running a bit late, you won't have to wait out in the weather."

Though she would rather meet anywhere but the Blue Bell for fear of running into Judd again, Callie bit her tongue. After all, he was the woman's son. It wouldn't do to offend her after she'd been so helpful. "That'll be fine. Thanks, Molly."

As soon as Molly closed the door behind Callie, she turned to face her son, her lips pressed tightly together. The look she wore warned Judd that if he was thirteen instead of thirty, she'd probably give his ear a good hard twist.

"And what was that all about?" she demanded to know. "I taught you better manners than that."

Judd flopped down on the settee and threw a leg up, sinking a boot into the velvet upholstery. He pulled his hat over his eyes. "She's a reporter, Mom."

"Callie?" When his hat moved in a nod, her lips thinned and she gave his boot a shove. His heel hit the floor at the same moment her hand whacked the hat off his head. "When you're in my house, the hat's off."

Judd bit back a smile as he looked up at her. "This isn't your house."

She pursed her lips in a frown. "Yours, either, but that isn't the point. How do you know she's a reporter?"

"Don't for a fact, but her back seat is full of cameras."

"Is that right?" Molly replied, her voice heavy with sarcasm. "And just because she has a few cameras you automatically assume she's a reporter?"

"That and the fact that she lied about why she's in Guthrie."

"Lied! She's here to trace some of her family. She told me so herself."

Judd snorted. "Mom, you know as well as I do that Mary Elizabeth Sawyer only had one child and that child died at birth. Callie Benson made up this cock-and-bull story about tracing some of her family to hang around town long enough to get a story about me. She just chose the wrong family to claim as kin is all."

Molly sagged down onto the rocker, knotting her fingers into her skirt's fabric. She was torn between knocking some sense in her son's head and gathering him up, big as he was, in her lap for a cuddle. But she knew comfort wasn't what he needed. He needed a shove, a good, hard shove to get him headed in the right direction. "When are you going to quit looking over your shoulder and live like a normal human being?"

"There's nothing wrong with the way I live."

"Not if you consider spending all your time with a dog normal."

"Baby would take offense at that."

"If Baby could talk, he'd tell you to quit hiding."

The conversation was old ground and Judd wasn't in the mood to travel it again. He rose to his feet, scooped his hat off the floor and shoved it back on his head. "I'm not hiding," he said tersely. "I came home is all, where I thought I could find a little peace." He strode to the door. "Thanks to Miss Callie Benson, it doesn't look like I'll be getting any of that."

He slammed the door behind him hard enough to rattle the pictures on the wall. Molly's heart twisted as only a mother's can as she watched him stride down the sidewalk. "Oh, Judd," she murmured sadly. "When are you going to climb out of that hole you've dug for yourself?"

Callie hurried to keep up with Judd's long stride. "I thought your mother was going to meet me."

"Yeah, well, she called and asked me to, instead. Has a migraine, she said." He stopped in front of the door Callie had passed the night before on her way to the Blue Bell. The smudge of her handprint where she'd cleared a spot to peek inside still appeared on its glass.

Judd stabbed the key into the door's lock and gave it a twist. "But understand—" he tossed over his shoulder "—I'm only doing this as a favor to her. If it were up to me, you wouldn't get near the place."

"I certainly didn't think you would do anything to help me," Callie replied in an equally snide voice.

The door opened with a screech of rusty hinges, and curiosity displaced irritation as she peered past Judd into the shadowed opening. No music drifted down to tease her and no shadows danced on the landing above, yet a chill chased down her spine, just as it had the night before when she'd stood before this same door.

She hugged her purse tightly against her breasts, unable to take that first step inside. "Do you believe in ghosts?" she murmured in a low voice.

Judd cut her a glance full of impatience. "No. Why?"

"Last night when I walked past here, I thought I heard music and voices coming from up there," she said with a nod toward the staircase that led to the second floor.

"Probably just the wind."

Callie stared up the steep flight of stairs and tried to convince herself he was probably right. Taking a deep, fortifying breath, she eased past him.

"Watch your step," he called from behind her. "I'll hit the lights."

At the top of the stairs, she stopped and waited. She stole a glance around, half expecting to see people dancing in the waning afternoon light. Instead, she found boxes, furniture, trunks and an assortment of junk stacked in odd-shaped piles around the room and shoved up against its walls. A fine layer of dust covered every surface while cobwebs draped the corners, giving everything a neglected, haunted look.

The lights came on and seconds later she heard the scrape of Judd's boots on the staircase behind her. The combination gave her the courage to wander farther into the room. "What is all this?" she asked as she dusted off a box lid and lifted it to peer inside.

"Junk. Some of it my parents inherited when they bought the building years ago. Some of it's family mementos and the rest belongs to the historical society. People are all the time donating stuff and mom has it hauled up here until she or one of the other members has time to go through it."

Callie wove her way through the piles until she noticed the unusual number of doors opening off the main area. "What was this place?"

"For years, nothing. Originally it was a whorehouse."

"A whorehouse," she repeated incredulous. Goose bumps popped up on her arms as she remembered hearing the woman's voice the night before, the voice that had called down for her to "Come on up and join us." She forced a laugh as she walked from door to door, peering into rooms only large enough to hold a bed. "Are you sure it still isn't used for that purpose?"

"Not that I'm aware of." Judd watched her from the center of the room, his eyes narrowed in suspicion, his arms folded across his chest. "And what do you plan to do up here?"

Callie ducked into an open doorway. "Set up a temporary studio," she said in a muffled voice.

"Studio? For what?"

She reappeared, wearing a smudge of dirt on her cheek. "Sculpting."

Judd snorted. "Sculpting? I thought you were here to trace your family history."

"That, too. But it looks like I'm going to be here longer than I expected, and I have a project I need to work on." She returned to the center of the room and turned in a slow circle, studying the afternoon light. "I'll probably do most of my work early in the mornings and evenings," she murmured half to herself.

With that in mind, she strolled toward the corner room which faced the street. The room contained two sets of windows, one facing south and one east. She folded her arms beneath her breasts, smiling her satisfaction. "Perfect." She turned to find Judd had followed her into the room. "How much is the rent?"

"By the hour?" he asked, lifting a brow.

Callie smothered a laugh. "By the month."

"A hundred dollars."

"I'll take it."

Judd tossed the check onto his mother's lap. "Here's the rent money."

Molly laid aside her needlepoint to pick up the check, smiling. "Good. I was hoping she'd take it."

Judd flopped down on the couch and stretched his feet out, eyeing his mother suspiciously. "I thought you had a migraine?"

Molly pretended to study the check, avoiding her son's gaze. "I did, but it's much better now, thank you."

Judd sucked in his cheeks as he watched his mother's face redden. She'd always been a lousy liar. "I'm sure it is," he muttered. "Why didn't you tell her the place was originally a whorehouse?"

Molly folded the check and slipped it into her pocket. "I didn't think it necessary."

"Not even when you consider the fact that her great-grandfather's mother was the madam?"

Molly's features softened in sympathy. "I thought the poor girl had suffered enough surprises for one day."

Judd threw up his hands. "Terrific! Now we have the great-great-granddaughter of Miss Lizzy, Guthrie's most famous madam, renting one of the old girl's rooms, and she doesn't even know it."

Molly looked down her nose at Judd. "Don't be disrespectful. Miss Lizzy was a fine, upstanding woman. Besides," she said with a sniff, "you said you didn't believe Callie was a descendant of Miss Lizzy's, anyway."

"Hell, I don't know what to think. Now she says she's an artist and she's going to use the space upstairs as a temporary studio while she's here."

"Maybe she is an artist."

"Yeah, and I'm an elephant trainer." Judd folded his arms across his chest. "And I suppose you're going to leave it up to me to tell her the truth?"

"Only when you think the time is right, dear." Suddenly Molly's eyes widened and her mouth dropped open. "That's it!" she cried. She rocketed from her chair, dropping her needlepoint to the floor while she made a beeline for an old rolltop desk, heaped high with stacks of paper. "I knew I recognized her name." She dug through the pile and came up with a brochure. "Callie Benson." She crossed the room and waved the brochure under her son's nose. "And you thought she was a reporter." She made a *tsking* sound with her tongue and tossed the brochure onto his lap. "She's an artist. A brilliant one, I might add. And now you've probably insulted her with your crazy suspicions."

Judd picked up the brochure and flipped through it while his mother paced in front of him, continuing her chastisement of him for his rudeness. He knew, given time, she'd wind down. She always did. While he waited for that to happen, he entertained himself by reading the brochure.

The pamphlet consisted of about seven pages, filled front and back with pictures of sculptures. The last page was the one that caught his attention, though. For on it was a picture of Callie, stooped over a mound of clay with the beginnings of a face appearing beneath her mud-slickened hands. If not for the picture, he could have ignored the brochure and her claim to be an artist as just one more lie.

"And I think you owe the woman an apology, at the very least."

An apology? Judd closed his eyes and hauled in a long breath, thinking an apology wouldn't even come close. Especially considering the way he'd treated her in her hotel room the night before. Maybe instead of offering an apology, he ought to just lie down and let her stomp on him for a while. Maybe then, she'd consider them even.

Callie sat on the floor of her hotel room with copies of magazine articles and newspaper clippings scattered all around her. Prudy, as always, had come through for her, faxing every word that had been written about Judd Barker over the last three years. Callie had scanned the reports monitoring his career climb, highlighted in yellow pertinent facts about him and stacked them to the side. The one thing that puzzled her was that he seemed to have given it all up. The career, the money, the fame. As far as she could tell, he hadn't cut a record or made a public appearance since the trial. Odd, but then he was an odd man, she thought.

The articles concerning the alleged rape and subsequent trial remained in front of her. She chewed the pen's plastic top as she glanced over the papers spread in front of her. The headlines that heralded his arrest were bold and front page.

The captions alone were enough to convict a man—if they were to be believed—and the photographs accompanying them, damning. Judd pictured leaning over the edge of a stage, kissing a woman. Judd grinning from ear to ear standing backstage surrounded by screaming fans, all of whom were female. Judd caught unaware in a bar, a lusty smile on his lips while his eyes were closed, his arms wrapped around a woman's waist while they danced cheek to cheek, groin to grinding groin.

"Disgusting," she muttered, yet picked the picture up to study it closer. He was wearing his black hat. Naturally. The brim was pulled low over his forehead, but not far enough to hide his face. The woman had poured herself over him like water and by the expression on Judd's face, he didn't seem to mind getting wet. In fact, his nose was buried in her hair and his lips a breath away from her ear.

Callie's fingers tightened on the picture, creating a crease across the dancing couple. A slow warmth spread through her abdomen. She remembered only too well how it felt to be held by him, the muscles in his arms rippling as they wrapped around her, his breath warming the skin at her throat.

She remembered his kiss, too. The feel of his lips pressed against hers, his taste. Like forbidden sex, she remembered. Wild and dark and passionate. Though she wanted to, she knew she would never forget.

A knock sounded at the door.

Her thoughts mired in memories of the man pictured before her, she called absently, "Who is it?"

"Judd Barker," came the muffled reply.

Callie's eyes widened, and she dropped the picture as if it had come to life in her hands. Quickly, she began scraping up the scattered papers. "What do you want?" she asked, stalling for time.

"I need to talk to you."

"What about?"

"Could you open the door?"

Grimacing, Callie lifted the bedspread and shoved the clippings between it and the sheets, then smoothed her hands to cover the conspicuous lumps. Straightening her clothes, she hurried to the door and opened it.

Slightly breathless, she looked up at him, hoping she didn't look as guilty as she felt. "Yes?"

He pulled off his hat and held it at his waist. "Mind if I come in?"

"I was just about to—"

"What I have to say won't take but a minute." Without waiting for permission, he strolled past her.

Frowning at his back, Callie closed the door. With Judd inside, the room seemed to shrink to at least half its size. She knotted her fingers, then unknotted them to gesture to a chair. "Would you like to sit down?"

He turned, slowly working the hat by its brim between his hands. "No, I'd rather stand, if you don't mind, and take my punishment like a man."

Callie stared, her forehead wrinkling in confusion. "What punishment?"

A sheepish grin chipped one corner of his mouth. "I hope nothing more serious than a tongue lashing, although my mother's already done a pretty good job with that." He dipped his head to stare at his hat, then lifted his gaze just enough to peer at her over his eyebrows. "Seems as if I owe you an apology. A big one."

Callie folded her arms at her breasts. "Oh?" she said, arching a brow.

"Yeah. I thought you were some sleazy reporter who'd tracked me down to write a story about me."

"And what made you think that?"

"The cameras in your car."

"What made you change your mind?"

"My mother. She showed me a brochure of yours. Some showing of yours in Dallas. Had pictures of your work and all."

Callie knew the one he spoke of. The showing had been less than a month ago and brochures had been mailed out to art dealers and patrons all over the country.

"As a result," she replied, "you've decided to believe that I'm in Guthrie only to trace my family?"

"The pictures seem real enough."

Callie narrowed her eyes at him. "You still doubt my intentions, though, don't you?"

When he didn't reply, she puckered her lips in a knowing frown. "I thought so."

Judd shifted uncomfortably under her steady perusal, not at all sure he was going to get the forgiveness he'd come for. In need of something to fill the silence until she softened a little, he offered, "Mom said you weren't leaving town until you found out the truth about the grave."

Callie started to sit down on the bed, remembered the papers she'd stuffed there and carefully skirted it. "That's my plan."

"Why is this so all-fired important?"

She wasn't sure how she could explain the importance or even why she should try, but for some reason she felt compelled to do just that. Opening a dresser drawer, she pulled out a thick leather album bound by a faded gold cord. "This belongs to my great-grandfather."

She flipped open the book and pointed to the first page, then held it out for Judd. "That is a picture of the Sawyer family. The young woman on the left is Mary Elizabeth. When she was nineteen, she ran away from home with a man her family didn't approve of and they disowned her. Approximately eight months after she left, the Sawyers received a telegram notifying them that their daughter had died in childbirth but that her baby had lived. Arrangements were made for the baby to be delivered to the Sawyers in St. Louis. They traveled there by train, picked up the baby and took him to their home in Boston and raised him.''

She flipped several pages and pointed again. ''This is a picture of my great-grandfather William Leighton Sawyer at the age of nine months. His grandmother, Mary Elizabeth's mother, is holding him. From what my great-grandfather has told me, his grandparents never forgave Mary Elizabeth for running away and bringing shame on the family. They never allowed the mention of her name in their home. When he was old enough to demand answers, he was told she was nothing but a selfish little trollop and it was his fault she was dead.

''The Sawyers were strict and unforgiving people. After living with them, my great-grandfather understood why his mother might have run away and he developed an empathy for her. Along with that, he carried the guilt that he was the cause of her death.''

She sighed. ''I came here at his request to take a picture of her burial spot and find out what I could about her and her life here.'' She felt the burn of frustrated tears and batted them back. ''I wish I'd never come. With what I've discovered so far, I tend to believe the Sawyers were right about their daughter. I hate to ruin Papa's image of her.''

Callie's anger and dislike of the woman surprised Judd, for he'd never known of anyone who'd disliked Miss Lizzy. ''You don't think much of the woman, do you?''

''And why should I? She was obviously as selfish and spoiled as her parents claimed. Otherwise, she would have kept her son with her and raised him herself instead of lying about her death and shipping her baby off to her parents to raise.''

''How do you know she lied about her death?''

''Well, it's obvious, of course. There's simply no other explanation.'' Callie saw the doubt in his eyes, and her shoulders sagged in frustration. "Look. I know you don't believe me, but I swear everything I've told you is the truth." With nothing else to offer other than her word and what little proof her great-grandfather had supplied her, she waited, silently watching for Judd's reaction.

He held the book in place and turned back to the first page, comparing the photographs. That they were old, was obvious, but as far as Judd was concerned the pictures didn't prove a thing. There were quite a few early settlers who came to the Oklahoma Territory in hopes of escaping or forgetting what they'd left behind. Mary Elizabeth Sawyer obviously had been one of them, for nothing was known of her prior to her arrival in Guthrie. Oh, there had been rumors, lots of them. But Judd wasn't a man to place much stake in rumors. He had heard enough about himself to know rumors were more often fiction than fact.

He tipped his head to look up at Callie. "If Mary Elizabeth's baby lived, how do you explain the grave out at Summit View?"

"I can't. That's why I'm staying here until I find out the truth."

"How do you plan to do that?"

"I don't know. I suppose I could hire a lawyer and have some type of legal document drawn to have the grave exhumed."

"Seems a little drastic, don't you think?"

"Do you have a better idea?"

Judd shook his head. "No. Not at the moment." Slowly, he closed the cover on the album, then laid it aside. Though his curiosity was aroused, this little nightmare wasn't his to deal with. All he needed was an acceptance of his apology from the woman to appease his mother, then he could go home and forget Callie Benson and her family's problems.

He dipped his head and shuffled his feet a moment before lifting his gaze to hers again. "Well, are you going to forgive me for the way I treated you?"

The eyes that met Callie's looked sincere enough, but dang it, a simple apology for all she'd suffered at his hand didn't seem quite fair.

Judd saw her hesitation and hoped to ease it by offering a teasing grin. "If you don't, my mother's going to have my hide."

Callie eyed him a moment, trying not to smile at the image of the petite little Molly Barker taking a piece out of her strapping son's hide. "I might consider accepting your apology," she replied thoughtfully.

Judd's brow puckered. "You might?"

"Yeah. I might." Her arms crossed at her breasts, Callie circled him, her mind ticking away at the possibilities. This man had insulted her at every meeting, treated her like a piece of dirt he'd scraped off his boot, yet for some crazy reason, his kiss haunted her, and Callie didn't have time for any more ghosts. The life of Mary Elizabeth Sawyer was enough to lose sleep over for the present.

"Words are cheap, Barker," she finally said. "I think I'd like something with a little more substance by way of an apology."

Feeling like a rabbit cornered by a hound, Judd turned also, keeping a watchful eye on her. "And what would that be?"

Callie stopped, blocking his path to the door as she looked up at him. "I want you to kiss me again."

Four

Judd's eyes widened. "You want me to what?"

"I want you to kiss me like you did last night."

His eyes narrowed to slits. "Why?"

Callie met his gaze squarely. "Let's just call it an experiment."

"What kind of experiment?"

She heaved a frustrated breath. "Do you want me to accept your apology or not?"

"Well, yeah, but—"

"No buts. Either kiss me or go tell your mother I wouldn't accept your apology."

Judd glanced around, half expecting to find a hidden camera or at the least a tape recorder, but saw nothing but a suitcase and a scattering of clothes. "A kiss," he repeated, returning his gaze to hers. "Just a kiss and that's all?"

"That's it."

He tossed his hat to the bed and sighed. "This has to be the craziest thing I've ever done."

He stepped up to her and placed his hands at her waist. "Are you ready?"

At his touch, Callie's breath knotted in her throat. "Yes," she murmured.

His face lowered, blocking the bedside lamp's soft light. Automatically, Callie closed her eyes and lifted her face to his. This is it, she thought. Her chance to prove to herself that Judd Barker's kiss was no different than any other man's. The passion she remembered from the night before, the yearning she'd attributed to it, was nothing but a product of her own overactive imagination.

But then his lips met hers and she lost the ability to reason. Warmth. Heat. A taste that made her thirsty for more. His kiss was everything she'd remembered, imagined... and more. Her lips parted in response to him.

Judd had meant to plant an innocent kiss, take his apology and get the hell out of Dodge. But something happened between intent and exit that kept him glued to that spot of carpet, his hands at her waist, his mouth pressed against hers.

He'd kissed a lot of women in his day, some whose names he couldn't even remember, but none with the passion this woman possessed. At the first touch, she had his heart slamming against his rib cage and his blood temperature shooting up about ten degrees.

An ache throbbed to life deep within him. To ease it, he caught her hips in his hand and dragged her close. He tasted as well as felt her moan of pleasure seconds before she tore her lips from his. The sting of disappointment at her withdrawal hit him sharp and fast.

She pressed her forehead to his, her chest heaving, her fingernails digging into his biceps. "I was afraid of that," she murmured.

"Afraid of what?"

She lifted her face, her eyes as wide and as full of fear as a rabbit's caught in a beam of headlights. "Afraid that it was as good as I remembered."

A chuckle rumbled low in Judd's chest. He didn't know if the reaction was from relief—to discover that she was as affected as he by the kiss—or the openness of her admission. Whatever the reason, he hugged her tight against him. "Did you expect less?"

"No," she whispered against his chest. "But I'd hoped."

He levered a finger beneath her chin and lifted, tipping her face up to his. The heat radiating from her eyes made his own burn in response. "Is the experiment over?"

Her lips trembled a one-word response. "Y-yes."

"And the results? Were they what you wanted?"

"Yes." She saw the flicker of knowledge in his eyes, telling her he knew she lied. Already regretting her impulsive request for him to kiss her, she dropped her gaze and swallowed hard. "No," she murmured.

"Maybe we should give it another try."

Her gaze flew to meet his. "No, please—" But his lips were already on hers. His hands slid down her back again to cup the cheeks of her backside. His knees bent slightly as he dipped to match the length of his body to hers. Desire sliced through her, sharp and biting.

He rolled his hips from side to side in a maddeningly slow rhythm, his groin rubbing against hers, the swell of his manhood as evident to her as the dig of his belt buckle against her waist.

Passion became something tangible, something she could taste, feel . . . a need that cried out for satisfaction. A sob welled in her throat.

This shouldn't be happening, she told herself even as her fingers moved to his chest. This man was all but a stranger. Stephen should be the one kissing her this way, Stephen who evoked these feelings in her. Nice, safe Stephen whom she'd known most of her life. Why couldn't *he* make her feel this way? Yet, she'd kissed Stephen a thousand times and not once had she ever wanted to fling aside convention and roll naked with him on the floor.

But she wanted to with Judd Baker. She wanted to go on kissing him until somehow he quenched this thirst. She wanted to feel his skin heat beneath her hands. She wanted to feel the strength of his muscles tighten against her bare skin. She wanted—God, how she wanted.

Judd wasn't sure what he wanted anymore. He'd thought it was to give her a kiss, get his apology accepted and get out, but that purpose was slowly going up in smoke to be replaced by a stronger desire to make love to this woman. And that was something that hadn't happened to him in a long time.

His hands still cupped at her buttocks, he lifted, inching her body up the length of his, until her toes cleared the floor. He held her against him, until the pounding of his blood eased in his ears, then slowly he crossed the short distance to the bed.

He braced first one knee atop the mattress, then the other and bent until she lay beneath him, his lips still melded to hers. He slipped his hands from beneath her and slowly eased his weight down until he stretched across her length. Knotting his fingers in the mahogany hair puddled at her shoulders, he pulled his lips from hers, holding himself upright by digging his elbows in the mattress.

He stared down into blue eyes glazed silver with passion for long seconds, searching for any sign of fear. When he didn't find anything but amazement, a slow smile curved one corner of his mouth. "Am I forgiven now?"

Callie closed her eyes. "Yes," she whispered, sure that now that he'd gotten what he'd come for, he would leave, but not at all certain that was what she wanted him to do.

"Good." He lifted a finger to move a strand of hair away from her face. "You know, you throw quite a punch."

She opened her eyes, surprised to find he didn't appear to be in any hurry to leave. "I beg your pardon?"

"Your kiss. I had to check twice to make sure my lips hadn't melted plumb off my face."

His comment was so unexpected, Callie sputtered a laugh, her breasts bobbing against his chest. "You throw quite a punch yourself."

"That a fact?" He eased off her to lay at her side while he allowed his fingers to drift to her shirt's top button. He felt the hitch in her breathing when his arm inadvertently rubbed across a turgid nipple. Rather than unbutton the button, he toyed with it, watching her chest rise and fall in increasing speed with each brush of his knuckles against her bare skin. Another time, he might have felt a swell of pleasure to know he affected a woman in such a way, but at the moment he was too busy trying to keep his hand from trembling to notice much else.

A year. A long, lonesome year without the pleasure of a woman's company, much less the release a man found with one. He shifted again, trying to ease the pressure building inside his jeans. He locked his hip when he heard the rustle of paper beneath him and the soft plop of something hitting the floor. He raised up to peer over the side of the bed.

Headlines glared up at him from papers scattered on the floor. Judd Barker Arrested After Raping Fan.

He doubled over as if he'd been shot. He clamped his hands over his face, blocking out the sight, but the images continued to slam at him. Flashing cameras, reporters shoving microphones under his nose, jeering faces. The humiliation, the pain...the loneliness.

No, he roared inwardly. *No!* Dragging his hands down his face, he stumbled to his feet. His boots ground against the papers in his haste to escape the unwanted reminder.

Without looking, Callie knew the cause of distress on Judd's face. That she was responsible for it, made her heart wrench in her chest. She rolled to a sitting position, her hand outstretched, reaching for him. "Judd, please," she begged. "I can explain."

He staggered to the door like a man wounded. "No. There's no need." He twisted open the door and, without looking back, said, "I'll have a key made for the room you rented and leave it at the front desk with Frank."

Afternoon sunshine warmed Judd's back through the plate-glass window behind him and threw an irritating glare on the pages of the liquor inventory he worked on. He slapped a hand to the back of his neck and rubbed at the tensed muscles there. Between the sun and the noise drifting down from upstairs, he was having a hell of a time keeping his mind on his order.

Judging by the amount of noise coming from above him, Callie had picked up the key he'd left with Frank. Shoving, dragging, scraping. Tall ceilings and hardwood floors magnified all the sounds and grated on the only good nerve he had left. He shoved back the chair, raking his fingers through his hair. "Jesus! What is she doing up there?"

From his post behind the bar, Hank shrugged and continued to polish glasses. "Don't know, boss. Sounds like she's destroying the place. Want me to see what she's up to?"

"No, I sure as hell don't." Judd dropped back down in his chair and began furiously shuffling the scattered pages back into a semblance of order.

Hank bit back a grin as he went back to his polishing. He hadn't seen his boss this worked up over a woman in longer than he cared to remember.

A loud thump shook the ceiling above them and both Judd and Hank tipped their chins upward, half expecting the ceiling to come crashing down on their heads. Judd stole a glance at the stairway that led to the second floor, thinking maybe he ought to go up and check on her. Growling under his breath, he hitched his chair beneath his rear end and scooted around the table until his back faced the staircase. No, he wasn't going upstairs. She could damn well fall through the ceiling and break her neck before he climbed those stairs.

He plopped his elbows on the table, clamped his hands over his ears and tried hard to block out the sounds coming from above as he squinted at the inventory in front of him. He'd done a pretty decent job of accomplishing just that when a huge crash sent debris crumbling from the ceiling and spattering his work. He would have ignored that as well, but unfortunately a blood-curdling scream followed it.

Judd and Hank both bolted for the stairway. Judd beat the other man by a good two strides. At the top of the stairs, Judd stopped, his gaze slicing across the room, searching for a sign of her. He saw her crouched against the far corner, hugging her arms to her breasts. Alligator-size tears streamed down her face.

"Callie!" He charged toward her, shoving boxes out of the way. He dropped to one knee in front of her. "Are you all right?"

She hurled herself into his arms, her fingernails digging into his biceps as she tried to climb up his body. Bracing himself to remain erect, Judd stood, bringing her up with him.

"Oh, God, it was awful," she cried, burying her face against his shoulder.

Shocked by the raw fear in her voice, Judd slowly eased an arm around her and awkwardly patted a hand to her back. "What was awful?"

"I was moving a box over there," she said, releasing her grip on him only long enough to point. "And this huge rat leapt out at me." A fresh wave of shudders shook her from head to toe, and she buried her face against Judd's chest.

"A rat?" he repeated, cutting a glance at Hank over the top of her head.

"Yes," she sobbed. "He was huge and ugly and had beady eyes and yellow teeth."

Hank turned his back to smother a laugh. "I'll go downstairs, boss, and find some mousetraps."

"Good idea," Judd murmured, wishing he'd thought of it first; then he wouldn't be cornered here with Callie in his arms. He continued to pat her on the back with one hand, while he dug the other into his back pocket. He pulled out his handkerchief and stepped back, dipping his knees to look at her face. "Better now?" he asked.

Her head bobbed slowly. He dabbed at the tears wetting her cheeks. "We'll set some traps and put out some poison tonight."

Her head bobbed again, her eyes riveted on his as she murmured a barely audible, "Thank you."

He took another step away, stuffing the wet handkerchief back in his pocket. "Well, I guess I'd better be getting back down to the bar."

Callie laid a hand on his arm to stop him. "Wait, please." His muscles tensed beneath her fingertips, and she withdrew her hand to clutch it with her other at her waist. "Thanks for coming to my rescue."

"No problem. That's what landlords are for." He started to turn away, but her voice stopped him.

"Judd? I'm sorry. Really I am."

He knew her apology had nothing to do with the rat or interrupting his work. She referred to the copies on the floor of her hotel room. He glanced away. "It's not important."

"Yes, it is. I know those articles drew memories you'd rather forget. It was my fault they were there and I'm sorry for that."

Though he would rather have dropped the subject and returned to the sanctuary of the bar, he had to ask one question—the one that had kept him up most of the night. Slowly, he lifted his head to look at her. "Why were those pictures hidden in your bed?"

"I was looking at them when you knocked. Rather than have you see them, I stuffed them under the bedspread."

Anger burned, tightening his throat and making his voice harsh. "Why'd you even have the damn things?"

"I was curious." Her face throbbed in embarrassment, but she knew she had to explain. After the pain she'd caused him, she owed him that much. "No one has ever kissed me the way you did, or made me feel that way before." She gathered her hands into a tight fist in front of her. "I just wanted to know something about you. That's all."

His eyes turned hard as steel. "So what do you think? Did I do it?"

Callie would rather climb in the hole the rat had found than answer the question. Since that wasn't a possibility, she offered vaguely, "I don't know."

"Surely you have an opinion after reading all the trash they published about the trial."

"If I were to judge on that alone, I'd say you were guilty." She waited a beat, then added, "But I learned a long time ago to believe only half of what I see, and none of what I hear."

He stared at her long and hard. "Yet you believe you are a descendant of Miss Lizzy's?"

"Miss Lizzy?"

"Mary Elizabeth Sawyer. That's what everybody in town called her."

"Oh," she replied thoughtfully, then more determinedly asserted, "Yes, I do."

"Why?"

"Because William Leighton Sawyer is my great-grandfather, and he was her son."

"Who says?"

"He says."

"And you believe him?"

"Yes!"

"Why?"

"Because I trust him."

Judd took a step toward her. "Do you trust me?"

Cornered, Callie took a step back. "Well, yes."

"Liar."

She stopped, and her chin came up. "Okay, I don't trust you, but then I don't know you as well as I do Papa."

"That I can accept. Because I don't know you, either, and I'm not at all sure I trust you." He puckered his lips thoughtfully. "I guess that makes us about even then, doesn't it?"

Callie's breath sagged out of her. For the first time since she had met Judd, she felt as if they were on even ground. "Yeah, I guess it does."

Judd stared at her for a moment, then nodded toward the boxes. "What were you doing when the mouse paid you a visit?"

"That was no mouse," she stated indignantly. "It was a rat, and I was trying to clear a path to the room I rented so I can move in my equipment."

"Need any help?"

The offer took Callie by surprise. "Well, yes, if you don't have anything else to do."

Judd thought of the liquor order spread on the table downstairs that was due in by five o'clock. If he helped her, he knew he'd never get it done in time. "Nothing that can't wait."

They fell to the task together, pushing and shoving, and a walkway soon appeared. While Judd dragged an old, tattered sofa out of the way and nudged it against the wall, Callie lifted the lid on a trunk. The stinging scent of mothballs hit her full in the face. Fanning the air beneath her nose, she lifted out a box. She opened it and poked through an assortment of buttons, yellowed envelopes and broken pieces of jewelry. She chuckled as she picked up a letter and waved it toward Judd. "Would you look at this? A three cent—"

Her smile faded when she caught a glimpse of the address.

Judd made his way through the trail of boxes, dusting off his hands. "What cost three cents?"

"A postage stamp," she murmured, her eyes fixed on the name.

When he reached her side, she lifted her gaze to his, her eyes filled with a mixture of excitement and apprehension, and handed him the envelope.

Frowning, Judd scanned the front of the envelope. *Mrs. Elizabeth Bodean, Guthrie, Oklahoma.* He glanced up to find Callie watching him through unblinking eyes.

"It was hers," she said, her voice barely above a whisper. "Mary Elizabeth's."

He'd known the trunk was here and more, but he hadn't told Callie. There were secrets he felt obligated to protect. Unable to meet her gaze any longer, Judd dropped his own back to the envelope. "So it is."

Callie sank to her knees in front of the trunk. "The answers I'm looking for might very well be right here."

"Maybe," Judd replied doubtfully.

Callie tipped up her head. "Do you think anyone would mind my looking through this?"

A disapproving frown quirked one side of Judd's mouth, but then he let out a sigh. "Who'd complain? The Bodeans didn't have any family. All this junk was here when my parents bought the building years ago." He watched her reach inside and knew this was something she needed to do on her own. "I'll head back downstairs. If you need anything, just holler."

Her attention already taken by the contents of the trunk, Callie replied absently, "Thanks, Judd."

Hours later, Callie sat curled on the tattered tapestry sofa, surrounded by piles of old clothes, stacks of yellowed letters bound by faded ribbon and boxes filled with sundry items whose importance were only known by the person who had placed them there. In her lap lay an opened book. An old floor lamp, dragged from one of the rooms opening off the common area, threw a circle of light on the book. Bound in leather and filled with the swirling handwriting of a young girl, the diary was the one Mary Elizabeth Sawyer had started at the age of sixteen.

Callie rubbed at her tired eyes and stretched to ease her cramped muscles. She'd read the entire book and didn't have any more idea than before about her great-great-grandmother—or Miss Lizzy, as Judd had said she'd been known.

The writings were those of a young girl, immature in many ways, but with a hint of the woman she must have become. That she was intelligent was obvious. That she was stubborn, more obvious still.

Callie sighed and laid the book aside. The answers she'd hoped to find still evaded her. The picture Lizzie had painted of her parents was much like that Papa had shared of his life with them. The Sawyers were cold, strict and unforgiving.

Her thoughts clouded by the past, she pulled a shawl up around her shoulders and leaned back, letting her mind drift. Why would a woman of Lizzy's upbringing leave Boston and follow a man she hardly knew halfway across the country into an unsettled and wild territory? And why had she sent her infant son back to Boston to be raised by the parents that by her own admission she'd wanted so badly to escape?

A door opened and closed, the sound seeming to come from one of the rooms behind her. Callie unfolded her legs and sat up, listening. A draft of cold air swept over her. She twisted around and squinted into the darkness beyond the lamp's circle of light. A shiver worked its way down her spine. She wrapped the shawl tightly around herself. "Is anyone there?" she called.

She strained to listen and watch. Shadows moved through the darkness, and Callie swore she heard a woman's voice humming a tender lullaby. She stood, took a few steps toward the far room, then stopped and listened again. The humming drifted away to be replaced by another sound coming from the opposite direction—the soft strains of guitar music. And it seemed to come from the staircase leading from the bar. Sure that the acoustics in the large room were playing tricks on her, Callie tiptoed to the stairwell and peered down.

The saloon had already closed for the night and only a single light shone above the bar. Drawn by the lonely call of each strummed chord, Callie eased down the steps and peeked over the stair rail, trying to locate the source of the haunting music. At the foot of the stairway, she turned, then ducked back into the shadows when she saw Judd sitting on a stool at the center of a small stage, a guitar propped on his knee. She waited, listening, letting the music wash over her until his thumb raked the strings on the final chord.

He continued to sit, his head bowed, his arm crooked lovingly over the guitar's curved body as if it were a woman's waist. Callie stepped from the shadows. "That was beautiful."

His head came up with a jerk. His eyes narrowed when he spotted her and he laid aside the guitar.

Though his look was anything but inviting, Callie strolled toward him. "I don't believe I've ever heard that tune before. What was it?"

"It's just a little ditty I've been working on."

"Are you planning to record it?"

"No."

"You should. It would be a hit."

"I'm not in the music business anymore." He pulled a cigarette from his front pocket, stuck it between his lips and let it dangle there while he stretched out a leg to dig a matchbook from his jean's pocket. The match flamed, illuminating his face behind his cupped hands. He looked the part of the gunslinger again, the lines on his face hard and unforgiving.

Callie watched him draw in the first long drag. "I didn't think singers smoked."

"They usually don't." He bent and picked up a beer sitting in a pool of condensation by his stool. Straightening, he tipped the bottle and drank long and deep. He lowered the bottle to his thigh and squinted at her through a haze of smoke. "But like I said, I'm not in the music business anymore."

He tilted the bottle her way. "Can I buy you a drink?"

Though she'd never developed the taste for beer, Callie shrugged. "Sure."

She followed him to the bar. He slipped behind it while she angled a hip onto a stool opposite him.

Judd pried the caps off two long-neck bottles and shoved one across the bar. Callie held hers between her palms, letting the moisture dampen her hands as she watched Judd lean back against the counter fronting the mirror. The light behind and above him threw his face into shadows. As always, simply being in his presence made her pulse race and her mouth go as dry as parchment. She lifted the bottle and took a sip.

She wasn't a beer drinker. Judd knew that as soon as he saw her nose wrinkle after the first delicate sip. Her tongue arced out to lick at the moisture the bottle had left around her mouth. He knew if he didn't say something and fast, he'd be tempted to kiss her again. "Did you find anything interesting in the trunk?"

The question won a frown. "No, not really. I found a diary Mary Elizabeth wrote as a teenager while still living at home with her parents, but nothing after her arrival in Guthrie."

"So what do you plan to do now?"

"I made an appointment with a lawyer for the day after tomorrow to check on having the grave exhumed."

Judd scowled.

His constant censure frustrated Callie. "I suppose you don't approve."

"No."

"May I ask why?"

"I think the past is sometimes better left alone."

The bitterness in his response could be a result of his own troubled history, but Callie had the distinct feeling he was holding something back. "Do you know something you aren't telling me?"

Judd stared at her a moment, his eyes shadowed and unreadable. "I've told you everything I know about the grave," he said finally. "Miss Lizzy's baby died at birth and was buried out on the hill at Summit View."

Callie's fingers tightened on the beer bottle. "Her baby did *not* die."

Judd pushed away from the counter and moved to lean across the bar, his face bare inches from hers. "I know. Her son's name is William Leighton Sawyer and he's one hundred and four years old and lives in a nursing home in Dallas." A teasing grin chipped at one corner of his mouth. "You sure are pretty when you're riled."

Heat flooded Callie's face at the backhanded compliment. She flattened her hand against his nose and shoved his face away. "Don't try to change the subject by sweet-talking me."

Judd chuckled. "Sorry, but you are pretty when you're riled." He flattened his palms on the bar, heaved himself up, then twisted around until his boots dangled next to Callie's knee. Catching her fingers in his, he lifted her hand, pulling her up until she stood between his legs. "How 'bout another little experiment?" he asked. "The last one we tried seemed a little inconclusive to me."

Five

"**D**o you mean a kiss, like the last experiment we tried?" she asked, her pulse skittering at the mere memory.

His lips curved in a lazy smile. "We could start there." He nudged aside her hair and brushed his lips across the sensitive skin beneath her ear. Callie dug her hands into his arms to steady herself. She didn't need another experiment. The first had been conclusive enough. Judd Barker's kisses devastated her like no other man's had. But if an experiment was what he needed to justify a little one-on-one, who was she to argue?

She closed her eyes and tipped back her head, savoring the warmth of his breath at her neck. "Okay," she whispered. "If you think it's necessary."

"Oh, I definitely think it's necessary," he whispered. He wet a trail up the smooth column of her neck with his tongue, then nipped lightly at her lower lip before withdrawing slightly to ask, "Don't you?"

"Yes," she murmured, forcing her eyes open to meet the heat in his eyes. "Yes," she repeated, then leaned into him, seeking the pleasure and taste of his lips again.

Judd locked his ankles beneath the cheeks of her backside and dragged her full against him, knotting his hands in her hair. Callie knew it was insane, impossible, but she wanted desperately to get closer still. She wanted to burrow beneath his skin and bury herself at the very core of his soul. The sensation was new to her, for she'd never experienced anything like it with Stephen. With him, she more often dodged intimacy than sought it. So why did she feel this way with Judd Barker, a man she barely knew? Why? Why? Why?

The question continued to hammer at her until she dragged her lips from his. Her breasts heaving, she framed his head between her hands and tipped his face until their foreheads touched.

"My God, how do you do this to me?" she murmured shakily.

"What do I do?"

Callie lifted her face until her gaze met his. "You make me crazy."

A hint of a smile touched his lips. "Do I? I thought it was you making me crazy."

"No," she said, wagging her head in denial. "It's definitely you." She took a step back, digging her fingers through her hair, confused by the emotions flooding her. "I think I should go."

Judd's eyes darkened and the smile slowly melted off his face. He hopped down from the bar. "Probably best if you did," he agreed curtly. "I'll walk you back to the hotel."

That she'd offended him was obvious, but it couldn't be helped. And she was about to offend him further, because she certainly didn't want him walking her back to the hotel. Distance is what she needed from him, not an escort.

"Thanks, but that's not necessary. The Harrison House is just a block away."

"It's late. You don't need to be out on the street alone."

One glance at the window and the eerie feeling she'd experienced earlier upstairs came crawling back. She swallowed back the arguments. "If you insist," she replied reluctantly, assuring herself she would leave him at the door to the hotel.

She followed him to the saloon's entrance, where he grabbed his duster and hat from a rack nearby before tugging open the door for her. Putting on her jacket, she stepped outside, then waited while he shrugged into his duster and locked up. Together, they started up the brick walk. They walked in silence, the night cold and lonesome around them. If she'd thought she could leave the magnetism that drew her to him at the bar, she was wrong. It hummed between them like something alive.

Their shoulders brushed once. Twice. Their knuckles grazed. Electricity crackled between them. Their hands touched again, and this time Judd laced his fingers through Callie's. Startled, she glanced up. His eyes remained fixed on the street ahead, his gaze unwavering, but he tightened his grip on her hand and lengthened his stride. Callie was forced to all but run to keep up.

By the time they reached the hotel, she was breathing hard, her skin alive with nerves. Judd pushed open the door to the hotel, nodded a tight-lipped greeting to Frank behind the desk and firmly guided Callie to the elevator. In silence, they traveled to the second floor, each staring at the floor indicator, unable and unwilling to look at the other. When the doors slid open, Judd slapped a hand against the panel to hold it open for her, then followed her out into the hallway.

Her fingers shaking, Callie dug her key from her jacket pocket. "Thanks for walking me to my room." She stuck the key in the lock and gave it a twist without looking at

Judd, though every nerve ending in her body tingled at his nearness.

"If I were a gentleman, I'd say good-night and go home."

Her heart leapt to her throat. Somehow she found the courage to look up. His eyes were on her, watching, waiting. The attraction that always seemed to hum between them turned to a deafening roar.

"I don't want you to go." The words were out before Callie could stop them.

Judd gave the door a push with the toe of his boot. "Good, 'cause I wasn't feeling like much of a gentleman."

Callie tore her gaze from his and entered the room ahead of him. A bedside lamp was on, bathing the room in soft light, and the bed covers were turned down, courtesy of the hotel. The room was spacious, but for some reason tonight the bed seemed to dominate the area. Callie cut a wide girth around it while she pulled off her jacket. She hung it in the closet, then reached for Judd's, her gaze meeting his, then skittering nervously away. She hung his duster beside her jacket, taking her good, sweet time at the task.

The weight of his hand at her shoulder made her turn. Their gazes met and tangled. Emotions warred in the depths of his brown eyes. Passion, loneliness, caution, even a little fear. Because she understood and shared each, her heart reached out to him.

He opened his arms in silent invitation and she stepped into them, wrapping her arms around his waist and laying her cheek against his chest. The thud of his heart was a welcome sound, the warmth and strength of his embrace a comfort she'd wanted more than she cared to admit.

Judd closed his eyes and rubbed his cheek against her hair, drinking in the scent and the silky texture. He'd missed the softness of a woman, the comfort and satisfaction of holding one close. He allowed himself the pleasure of doing just that until he felt her breath ease out of her on a soft sigh. Tucking a finger beneath her chin, he tilted her face up to his. "I want to make love with you."

She lifted her hands to his cheeks and drew his face to hers. "It scares me to death, but I want that, too," she whispered, then touched her lips to his.

Though his body trembled with his need for her, Judd let her set the pace, taking only what she was ready to offer. When she deepened the kiss, he hooked his arms in a loose embrace at the small of her back. He bit back a groan as she arched to meet him.

Needing to feel the full heat of her body against his, he dropped his hands to the cheeks of her backside and pulled her flush against him. He moved his hips in a slow, sensual dance, his belt buckle clicking against the brass studs on her jeans. Fearing he would bruise her, he unhooked the buckle and stripped the leather strap through the loops of his jeans. Metal clanked dully as he dropped it to the floor at their feet.

Holding her to him with nothing but the pressure of his mouth against hers, he fumbled with the buttons of his shirt as he tugged his shirttail from his jeans. He shrugged out of it and tossed it to the floor behind him. Impatient for the feel of her, he fitted his hands at her waist and lifted until her toes cleared the floor. Groaning, he crushed her to his bare chest.

The rub of her sweater frustrated as much as it appeased. He wanted to feel the softness of her skin, lose himself in her feminine swells and curves, drown in her seductive scent. Slowly he lowered her to her feet. Slower still he dragged his lips from hers. Holding her motionless with the strength of his gaze, he caught the hem of her sweater and pulled it up and over her head. Fighting to keep the tremble from his fingers, he unclasped the front closure of her bra and peeled it off her shoulders and down her arms. Pebbled by the cool air, rose-tinted nipples tipped upward, begging for his touch. His breath caught in his chest and burned.

Mesmerized by her beauty, he cupped a porcelain breast, taking its weight in the palm of his hand. Callie inhaled sharply, her breasts swelling, skin against heated skin. He lifted his gaze to hers, then laid a thumb against a nipple and rubbed the turgid peak, watching as the passion built on her face. Her eyes closed and her head fell back. She clasped her hands around his forearms to steady herself.

Hunger grew, gnawing at him, demanding immediate satisfaction, but he fought it back. He wanted to savor each moment, each taste, each sensation. He gathered Callie close, burying his face in her hair, taking in deep breaths to slow the urgency. It was a mistake, for with each breath her scent surrounded him, the fragrance of wildflowers crushed between a man's hands. He found her lips, and her taste nearly brought him to his knees. Hot, sweet, enticing. Holding her close, he walked backward until his legs hit the bed. He fell across it, taking her with him.

Callie heard a boot hit the floor, then a second. A toe nudged at her foot, found her heel and pushed off her loafer. Her second shoe fell to join the other of its own accord. She flattened her hands against his broad chest, absorbing the thunder of his heart and letting the heat permeate her skin. She molded her hands, tracing and setting to memory the shape of his chest, the strength of his shoulders.

She was only distantly aware of his movements as he shimmied out of his jeans, but when he moved his hands to the snap on hers, she shivered in anticipation. Frustrated as much as he by the clothes that separated them, Callie lifted her hips. Judd rose to his knees above her, caught her jeans in his hands and peeled them down her legs. He tossed them to the floor, then rose above her like a proud conqueror.

The artist in Callie cried out for her clay so that she could capture him just as he appeared at that very moment—with perspiration beading his skin and turning it bronze in the soft lamplight. Every muscle pumped with passion, accentuating the breadth of his shoulders, the bulge of his biceps and thighs, the tapered waist and narrow hips. Virility pulsed from every fiber of his being.

Callie opened her arms, welcoming him. Judd sank against her on a sigh.

To Judd, making love to a woman was much like making music. Both had a rhythm and a song, silently waiting for the touch of his fingers to bring it to life. He sought the music in Callie, playing his fingers over her breasts, down her rib cage, dipping them between her legs, then dragging them back across her heated skin in a rhythm that thrummed silently within him. He heard each tiny gasp of delight, every moan of pleasure, each whispered urging, and reveled in the passion buried within her.

Positioning himself above her with a knee on either side of her hips, he reached out, curving his hands around her breasts, tipping them upwards, then reshaping them in the gentle curve between thumb and finger. He strummed a nail across each tightened bud, watching while her face contorted then softened and a low moan of pleasure rumbled deep in her throat.

Unable to resist, he dipped his head first over one nipple, then the other. He flicked his tongue over each before drawing her breasts together between his hands and taking both nipples into his mouth, alternately sucking and laving until her body bucked against his.

Over and over again he brought her to the edge of insanity, then soothed her with gentle hands and tender words, until she lay panting, her body quivering with her need for him.

"Judd, please," she cried. "I want—"

Though he knew what she wanted, felt it in every shudder of her body against his, he had to hear her say it.

"What?" he whispered, raining fevered kisses from ear t
ear. "What do you want?"

Catching his cheeks between her hands, she forced hi
gaze to hers. "I want you," she whispered.

The truth of that darkened her eyes, empowering hin
with her trust—the one thing he'd needed before making he
his. He rocked back on his knees and caught her hips be
tween his hands. He drew her to him, slowly losing himsel
in the velvet wetness. He clenched his teeth and threw bacl
his head, groaning at the exquisite torture of being sur
rounded by her.

Callie arched against him as shock waves of pleasure rip
pled through her. He held her hips tight against his until the
ripples passed. Then he began to move inside her, slowl
setting the rhythm for her to follow.

With each thrust of his groin, he increased the tempo un
til perspiration beaded his skin beneath her clever hands
and his breath heaved hot and wanting between them. A
low, primal growl rose from deep within him as the pres
sure built. He dug his hands into her hips and arched har
against her, calling out her name as he took her with hin
over the edge.

Judd opened one eye to find sunshine bathing the room
He opened the second and cocked his head, slowly focus
ing on the woman curled against him. Her hair, polished to
the color of mahogany by morning sunshine, tumbled acros
the pillow and spilled over his arm and chest. Beneath the
burnished strands, her hand was tucked between her cheek
and his chest. Her other hand was buried somewhere unde
her pillow. She slept like she made love…with trust and tota
abandon.

Callie. Callie. Oh, Callie. Her name played through hi
mind again and again, like the refrain of a favorite song. Hi
breath eased out of him on a heavy sigh. He'd made love to
a lot of women in his day, and suffered through that morn-

ing-after awkwardness when they each went their separate
ways. But he'd never awakened with a knot of fear lodged
in his chest, dreading that moment of separation. In one
night, Callie had chipped her way through the walls he'd
erected around himself and burrowed her way into his heart.

He sighed again, then shifted to tuck a lock of hair behind her ear, giving him a better view of her face. Her eye-
lids twitched at his touch, and he held his breath. He didn't
want her to awaken just yet, for he didn't want their time
together to end. Time was something they didn't have. Once
she solved the mystery surrounding her great-grandfather's
birth, he knew she'd leave—for what would keep her in
Guthrie? A woman like her would smother and die in a
small town like this. She needed the big city with all its cul-
ture and color. Dallas was her home and much more her
style.

He tensed as his mind clicked to another possibility. Was
there someone in Dallas waiting for her return, even now?

In spite of him willing them otherwise, her eyes slowly
blinked open and her gaze met his. She smiled sleepily.
"Good mornin'," she murmured and cuddled closer.

"It is that," he agreed, snuggling her up higher on his
chest. "Did you sleep well?"

"Like a rock."

Judd chuckled. "Me, too." He traced a line from her
shoulder to her hip. She was here with him, had spent the
night in his arms, yet he couldn't shake the worrisome
thought about her leaving soon or the possibility of someone awaiting her return.

They hadn't discussed their pasts. There hadn't seemed to
be the need or even the time for that. But now he was curious and not sure how to raise the question.

"Is there a husband or a boyfriend who might come gunning for me?" he finally asked.

Callie lifted her head and looked at him. He thought he
caught a glimmer of apprehension in her eyes, but then she

laughed and tucked her head back against his chest. "A little late to be asking that question, don't you think?"

Callie sat on a scarred barstool, her stockinged toes curled around its rungs, her chin resting in her hand. Before her, a lump of terra-cotta clay and an armature rested on an old formica-topped kitchen table. Both the stool and the table she'd bought for a bargain at a used-furniture store a couple of blocks from the Harrison House. A drape of plastic sheeting protected a second smaller table "borrowed" from the whorehouse's main storage room. A plant mister, a scrub brush, several different sized bristle brushes, pieces of wire screen and her modeling tools awaited her use on its top.

It had taken her less than two hours to set up her temporary studio. She'd spent at least two more hours staring at the clay, waiting for inspiration to strike. The deadline for the sculpture for the Houston hospital's new women's pavilion was a scant six weeks away.

She shifted on the stool and let out a sigh. So far the clay remained untouched, her hands clean and inspiration something she feared she might never experience again. Knowing the statue wouldn't form itself, she broke off a large chunk of clay. She scooted her stool closer to the table and began to work the clay between her hands, warming it and softening it.

In her mind's eye, she saw the completed piece. A mother cradling a sleeping infant to her cheek. She'd never given birth herself, but she could imagine the emotions that would fill a mother's heart when holding her newborn for the first time. Pride. Love. Thankfulness. All mixed with a measure of awe. Each emotion she wanted reflected on the mother's face of the finished piece.

Unfortunately, the ability to produce the emotions in the clay escaped her, just as they had at her studio in Dallas. She had hoped that by getting away from Dallas and Stephen, the creative juices would flow.

They hadn't.

Her shoulders drooped. Maybe Prudy was right, she thought despondently. She'd said that Callie's creative block had nothing to do with her relationship with Stephen, but more with her relationship with her mother. She'd argued that Callie couldn't possibly be expected to create something she'd never experienced as a child from her own mother. Granted, Prudy tended to blame every problem in Callie's life on her mother, but this time Callie could see her point.

Although Frances Sawyer Benson possessed a great many admirable qualities, maternal love certainly wasn't one of them. Callie couldn't remember ever being cuddled by her mother, or ever hearing her mother say I love you. Throughout her life, Callie had struggled to earn her mother's attention and admiration, but she'd never received anything but her constant disapproval.

Papa was aware of Frances's shortcomings and had always told Callie her mother had inherited every drop of her cold-bloodedness from the Sawyer side of the family. After reading Lizzy's journal, Callie had a new understanding for that coldness and was inclined to agree.

The thought of the Sawyers and the journal channeled Callie's thoughts further to Lizzy. Had Lizzy shared the same traits as her mother? Evidently she had, she decided. How else could she have sent her infant son away?

Callie squeezed the clay in her palm, groaning. Coming to Guthrie certainly hadn't opened her creative juices. If anything, coming to Guthrie and discovering her great-great-grandmother's secret life had further stymied her ability to create.

The sound of a bark drew her thoughts from her work. She set aside the clay and moved to peer out the window. Across the street, Baby romped on winter brown grass. Judd sat on a park bench, his legs stretched out in front of him, teasing Baby with a ball. He'd pretend to throw it, hide it behind his back, then laugh when Baby bolted and spun in fast circles looking for the ball.

Her throat tightened and she lifted a hand to lay her fingertips against the cold glass. Her inability to evoke visions of motherhood might be blamed on her mother, but her distraction from her work today could be blamed on the man outside, as well.

What was it about him that drew her? she wondered. Was it purely sexual attraction? She'd definitely felt the tug from their first meeting. But, no, she told herself, beyond the physical there was something else. An unexplainable comfortableness that made being with him easy, as if they'd known each other for years.

Silly, because she didn't know him, not in the way she knew Stephen. Yet, when he looked at her, she didn't see a stranger, she saw a man, familiar and irresistible. And when he touched her, she didn't feel violated as she did sometimes with Stephen. She felt . . . she felt loved.

Her fingers curled against the windowpane at the thought. Loved? How could she possibly feel loved by someone she barely knew? Someone who, by all rights, she should fear?

A knot of apprehension tightened in her stomach. She stared at Judd, trying to fit the allegations that shadowed his past to the man innocently playing with his dog below. Nothing matched. Nothing. Judd Barker was a gentle man, a kind man. He'd never harm anyone, much less a woman.

Hadn't he proven that last night? He'd told her pointblank he'd wanted to make love with her, and in so doing, had placed the decision at her feet for her alone to make. If she hadn't been willing, he would never have forced himself on her. She knew that as surely as she knew her name. And he'd given of himself unselfishly, always conscious of her comfort, her needs, without her ever having to voice them.

While she watched, he lifted the ball and hurled it, sending Baby off at a run. He tossed back his head and laughed, the sun bright on his face, the wind whipping at his dark hair. Emotion knotted in her chest.

At that moment, Judd glanced up and caught Callie's eye. A grin spread across his face, slowly unraveling the knot in her chest. While she watched, he turned a thumb to his chest, pointing at himself, then joined his thumbs and index fingers in the shape of a heart. Without moving his gaze from hers, he slowly lifted a hand to point at her.

A sheet of glass, two stories and a street separated them, yet she felt the heat of his gaze as if they stood nose-to-nose. A warmth slowly spread through her as she watched him push himself to his feet and put on his hat. She couldn't hear his words, but knew he called Baby because the dog snapped up the ball and raced back to Judd's side. Judd scruffed Baby behind the ears then took the ball from him and shoved it into the pocket of his duster before heading across the street.

Callie's pulse kicked in anticipation, knowing he was coming to see her. Anxious to see him as well, she turned from the window, then wheeled about when she caught a glimpse of a sleek, silver car sliding into a parking space across the street. She stood motionless, her eyes fixed on the car as a tall, well-groomed man stepped to the curb and paused to look around.

She closed her eyes and pressed her forehead to the window. "Oh, no," she murmured.

"Excuse me, please. Could I ask directions of you?"

Impatient to see Callie, Judd started to ignore the request, but inbred courtesy made him turn and wait while the man who'd called to him jogged across the street. The guy looked like a Philadelphia lawyer with his three-piece suit,

Italian silk tie and slicked-back hair. In a country town like
Guthrie where boots and jeans were standard wear, he
looked as out of place as a turd floating in a punch bowl.
Judd craned his neck to check out the license plates on the
man's car. *Texas.*

"What can I do for you?" Judd asked, his voice guarded.
Baby growled low in his throat as the man approached, and
Judd placed a warning hand on the dog's collar.

"I'm looking for the Harrison Hotel," the man replied,
breathing heavily.

A jog across the street and the guy was already winded.
To Judd's mind, his endurance fit his image. He jerked his
head in the direction the man had just driven. "You just
passed it. A block east on the corner."

The man turned and looked. "So I did." He chuckled.
"A town this small, I'm surprised I missed it." He shook his
head, still chuckling. "To be honest, I'm lucky the town is
so small. Made it a hell of a lot easier to find the hotel where
my fiancée's staying."

A thread of apprehension tightened Judd's neck. "Oh?"

"Yes, she scampered off at the request of her great-
grandfather to trace some of the family who once lived here
and forgot to mention where she was staying. The old man's
crazier than a loon. When I had my secretary call him and
ask where she was planning on staying, he didn't even remember he had a great-granddaughter. Took my secretary
a while to trace down the hotel, but once she did, I thought
I'd drive up and surprise Callie."

Callie! The name ripped through Judd's heart like a rusty
knife and he stiffened at the pain. It took a moment for him
to find his voice. When he did, he replied dryly, "Oh, I'm
sure she'll be surprised." He touched a finger to the brim of
his hat. "Enjoy your trip to Guthrie." He slapped a hand to
his thigh. "Come on, Baby."

* * *

Callie flew down the stairs, stuffing her arms through her jacket's sleeves. She had to reach Judd before Stephen talked to him. She had to.

She jerked open the door and bolted outside only to see Judd walking away. "Judd!" she cried and started after him. A hand grabbed her from behind.

"Callie!" Stephen whirled her around and into his arms. "I was on my way to your hotel to find you."

Over Stephen's shoulder she watched Judd continue down the sidewalk toward the Blue Bell, his shoulders hunched, his hands buried deep in his duster's pockets. Baby trotted at his side, his snout tipped up, looking quizzically up at his master. She knew she was too late. Judd and Stephen had already met.

She wanted to call out to Judd, to beg him to stop so she could explain, but she knew this wasn't the time. Oh, why hadn't she told him about Stephen that morning when he'd asked if she had a husband or boyfriend who'd be gunning for him?

But she hadn't, and she couldn't change that now. Stepping from Stephen's embrace, she forced a smile. "Were you?"

"Yes," he said, puckering his mouth in a childish pout. "Which was no easy task to locate, considering you didn't tell anyone your whereabouts. You might have returned my calls," he added, sounding hurt.

Callie dug her hands into her jacket pockets to avoid further contact. "I told you I needed time alone."

It was so like Stephen: he ignored her withdrawal and wrapped an arm around her shoulders and turned her toward the hotel. He dipped his head close to her ear and said, "Which is exactly why I'm here."

Fiancée. Judd tightened his hand on the ball in his pocket and squeezed for all it was worth as he headed for the Blue

Bell Saloon. It was either that or put a fist through the brick wall beside him, and he valued his hands too much to risk that.

Why hadn't she told him she was engaged? he raged inwardly. She'd had the chance. He'd asked her point-blank that very morning if there was anybody he should worry about. She'd laughed his question off, making a joke of it.

But she hadn't given him an answer.

He had his answer now, though. Thanks to the unexpected appearance of the Philadelphia lawyer.

Hours later Judd climbed the carpeted stairs leading to the Sand Plum restaurant where he was to meet his mother and other members of the Historical Society to discuss an upcoming fund-raiser. Judd didn't want to go to the dinner meeting. He'd prefer to spend the evening at the Blue Bell, drowning his disappointment in a beer. But his mother had called, reminding him of the meeting, and if he'd refused to go she would've known something was up. To keep her off his back and out of his private life, he'd chosen to make a token appearance at the Sand Plum.

They'd arrived before him, all familiar faces, all smiling expectantly when they saw him. He crossed to the table and pulled out the chair beside his mother. Molly immediately pushed a salad plate in front of him and leaned toward him. "You're late," she whispered. "I ordered for you."

Judd pushed the plate away. "I got tied up at the bar."

Molly looked at him curiously. "Aren't you going to eat your salad?"

She had that look on her face that said if he refused, she'd put a hand to his forehead and check his temperature. At the moment, he didn't need or want any coddling. He dragged the salad plate back in front of him and picked up his fork.

Satisfied, Molly patted his arm. "We were just going over the details for the fund-raiser." She pushed on her glasses and shuffled through a scattering of papers. "The auditorium at the Masonic Temple is reserved for the night of December twentieth. The publicity will be taken care of by Myrna. Eddy is arranging for tickets and concessions." She pulled off her glasses and settled back against the padded chair. "That only leaves the entertainment." She turned her gaze full on Judd. "We're still hoping you'll agree to sing."

Carefully, Judd laid down his fork. "I talked to Casey Hubbard's manager. Casey's agreed to come and bring a few friends. She'll draw a good crowd."

"So would you."

Judd set his jaw as he sought patience. They'd already discussed this, many times, and his answer was always the same. An unqualified *no*.

Hoping to divert his mother's attention, he rubbed a hand across his stomach. "What did you order me for dinner? I'm starving."

"A steak and—" Her eyes brightened as she leaned to peer around Judd's shoulder. "Oh, look who's here."

Before he thought better of it, Judd turned. Callie stood at the hostess table with Stephen at her side. Stephen was dressed much as he had been when Judd had seen him earlier, only the color of his suit and tie had changed. Callie, though, looked like a snow angel, wearing a sweater dress of winter white with hose and heels of the same color. Her mane of hair was twisted high on her head, leaving tendrils feathering her cheeks, forehead and neck. An intricate dangle of pearls and gold dripped from each earlobe.

When Stephen spotted Judd, he raised a hand in recognition. He placed a hand at the small of Callie's back and guided her toward their table. The stab of jealousy Judd experienced upon seeing them was quickly replaced by the burn of betrayal.

As the two approached, the men at Judd's table rose, and he did as well, pushing out his chair and tossing his napkin to the table.

Stephen stuck out his hand, smiling. "So we meet again. Stephen Millage," he said by way of introduction.

"Judd Barker."

Recognition flashed in Stephen's eyes. Whether the recognition was from the name or the tawdry reputation surrounding the name, Judd didn't know and didn't care.

"The country music legend?" At Judd's curt nod, Stephen smiled. "I've never met a Grammy winner before. Wait until the secretary pool at the office hears this."

Judd withdrew his hand and cut a quick glance toward Callie. If anything, she looked as miserable as he felt.

Stephen angled himself to include Callie in the introductions. "I'm sorry. This is the young woman I was telling you about earlier, my fiancée, Callie Benson."

Judd waited, silently praying she'd deny the tag. When she didn't, he tore his gaze from hers. "We've met."

Stephen chuckled, oblivious to the tension stretched between the two. "In a town this small, I guess you would have bumped into each other by now."

Judd shifted his gaze to the others at the table and quickly made the necessary introductions.

Always the gracious hostess, Molly asked, "Would you two like to join us?"

Silent up to this point, Callie quickly intervened. "Oh, no. We wouldn't want to interrupt your dinner, but thank you." She caught Stephen's coat sleeve and backed away, tugging him with her.

Stephen lifted a hand in a parting wave. "It was nice meeting you all." His gaze settled on Judd. "Maybe we'll see each other again before I leave town."

Six

"Imagine finding a five-star restaurant in a hick town like this. Amazing, isn't it?"

"Guthrie isn't a hick town," Callie said defensively, forgetting that she herself had referred to it with the same words less than a week ago. But a lot had happened in that week to change her view of Guthrie. She'd developed an appreciation for the small town and its residents, enjoying the slower pace and the friendliness. "It's charming and full of history."

Stephen took the key from her hand and unlocked the door. "My fault, dear. A poor choice of words. Guthrie is a charming community."

Callie ground her teeth. Why did he always have to agree with her? Why couldn't he just once have an opinion of his own and stick with it?

She strode past him as soon as he pushed open the door. "We need to talk," she said, leaving him to follow or be left behind. He carefully shut the door, then dropped the key onto the dresser. While Callie hung her coat in the closet, he shrugged out of his and draped it over the back of a chair before sitting down.

Callie kicked off her shoes and plopped down on the bed, pulling her feet under her. Stephen sat opposite her, his elbows on the chair's arms, his fingers templed, patiently waiting as always for her to take the initiative.

She heaved a frustrated breath. "Stephen, why did you come here?"

His forehead crinkled quizzically. "To see you, of course." He added a sheepish smile. "And hopefully to persuade you to set a wedding date."

"You could have saved yourself the trip." Callie heard the sharpness in her reply and saw its effect on Stephen. Knowing he didn't deserve the brunt of her anger, she closed her eyes and fought for calm. "I'm fine, Stephen, as you can well see. And as I told you in the note I left, I'm not ready to set a date. I need time alone to think all this through."

His elbows remained on the chair's arms, his fingers templed. Only one brow arched, acknowledging that he'd heard what she'd said. Slowly, he lowered his hands. "You feel pressured," he said, always the placater. "And I can certainly understand why, considering the stress you've been under while working on this project for the Houston hospital."

"It's not the hospital project, Stephen."

"Your mother, then," he said, grasping for an excuse, anything to delay what he feared she was trying to tell him.

"No, it's not Mother." Callie heaved a sigh and plucked at a loose thread on the bedspread. "It's me, Stephen. Or rather, us." She glanced up, her gaze colliding with his. Pain darkened the familiar blue eyes looking at her, making her fight back waves of guilt. "Stephen, you're a wonderful man, kind beyond words and a dear friend. But I—I'm just not sure."

His expression went from pain to disbelief. "Not sure? What about all our plans? Our future?"

"*Your* plans, Stephen, not mine."

"But we've been friends for such a long time."

"Is friendship enough for you?"

"Friendship is an excellent basis for marriage."

"Yes, I realize that. But there has to be something more."

He sat silently, then rose and crossed to her. He sat down on the bed and took her hand in his. Slowly, he lifted it, pressing the back of her hand to his lips. "I'm sorry, dear. I forget a woman's need for romance."

Tears burned her eyes at the tenderness, yet the futility of the gesture. "Oh, Stephen," she murmured, cupping the back of his neck with her hand.

He lifted his face, his gaze on hers, then leaned toward her. Instinct had Callie tensing. His lips touched hers, and Callie forced herself to accept his kiss. She sat still, unmoving while his tongue probed, his hands groped for her breasts. She willed herself to feel something. Anything. The increase of her heartbeat. The thud of her pulse. A quickening in her lower region. Anticipation. Lust.

But the only feeling that stole over her was one of revulsion.

She dragged her lips away, dipping her chin to her chest. "Please, Stephen, don't."

Immediately contrite, he said, "I'm sorry, Callie. My timing's all wrong. You're tired, I'm sure, and so am I after that long drive." He rose, patting her hand with an understanding she felt she didn't deserve. "We'll talk in the morning when we're both fresh and rested."

Callie knew she was once again avoiding a final resolution to their relationship, for her feelings had nothing to do with being tired or Stephen's timing being off. But at the moment, all she wanted was for him to leave so that she could find Judd. She remained silent as Stephen collected his coat and prepared to leave.

At the door he paused. "Good night, Callie."

"Good night," she murmured. When the door closed behind him, she ripped her dress over her head, her hose down her legs and pulled on a warm pair of sweats.

Inky darkness urged Callie to a faster gait as she headed toward the Blue Bell. "Please be there," she murmured, her breath tangling with the cold air and forming puffs of vapor to drag behind her. She had to talk to Judd. She had to see him, touch him, feel the strength and reassurance of his arms around her.

She had to explain Stephen's unexpected appearance and tell him that she wasn't and never had been Stephen's fiancée.

At the entry to the Blue Bell, she twisted the door handle and found it locked. In frustration, she sagged against the door, her fingertips and nose pressed against the door's oval glass. Her breath fogged the etched pane. Through it a single light shone above the bar. The rest of the room hung in shadows. She dropped her arms to her sides as she stepped from the door. He was gone. A sob caught in her throat as she turned back for the hotel.

Her head bent, her shoulders hunched miserably against the cold, she retraced her steps, her shoes scuffing along the brick walk.

Cal-lie. Cal-lie.

Her head came up and her steps slowed at the searching quality in the call. She stopped in front of the door to the whorehouse and listened.

Cal-lie. Cal-lie.

The voice that called out to her was that of a woman, her whispered urging as mysterious and illusive as the wind.

Callie glanced around. "Who's there?" she called, her lips quivering.

She listened, straining to hear the voice again, but all she heard was the whine of the wind as it whistled through the eaves overhead. She turned her gaze on the door to the whorehouse. Darkness gaped beyond the glass. Stepping back to the edge of the curb, she craned her neck, looking upward toward the second floor. A light shone from her workroom window.

She hadn't left a light on, she remembered in rising apprehension. She hadn't even been in the building since Stephen had arrived earlier that day. While she watched, a shadow moved across the glass. Her heart leapt to her throat. Was it Judd? she wondered, already digging the keys to the building from her jacket pocket.

Her hand froze with the key buried in the lock. What if it isn't Judd? she thought with a stab of fear. What if it was some vandal or maybe a street person looking for a warm place to spend the night? Whoever it was, she told herself, she had to know and find out what they were doing in her workroom. She unlocked the door and gently eased it open. Darkness sucked at her, drawing her farther in.

Not knowing what or who awaited her, she braced her hands on either side of the wall and cautiously worked her way up the steps. At the top of the landing, she paused, listening as she looked around. Her heart hammered in her ears, deafening her to any other sound.

Seeing the door to her workroom open, she tiptoed across the floor and peeked inside. The room was empty but for the furnishings and equipment she'd moved in earlier. Her tools lay on the table where she'd left them, the mound of clay shrouded by the plastic she'd hastily draped over it. Just as she turned to leave, the interior door connecting her room to the one next to it squeaked open. Holding her breath, she watched a broad and decidedly male shoulder appear.

Having no weapon to protect herself with, she let out a blood-curdling scream and threw herself against the door, trying to lock the intruder on the other side.

"Jeez, Callie! It's me, Hank."

At the sound of the familiar voice, Callie released her hold on the door and slumped back against the wall, pressing a hand over her pounding heart.

She came off the wall when Hank pushed his way through the door. "You nearly scared the life out of me!" she yelled at him, fisting her hands at her hips.

Hank kept his back to her, and angled his head in such a way to avoid eye contact. "You didn't do such a bad job on me, yourself."

"How did you know it was me out here?" she demanded, irritated that he'd frightened her.

He chuckled. "That scream. I've heard it before."

Reminded that he had responded with Judd to her hysterical reaction to the rat the day before, Callie's cheeks heated in embarrassment. "Oh." When he continued to stand with his back to her, though, her suspicions returned. "What are you doing up here, anyway?"

"N-nothing." He tucked his hand behind his back as he turned to face her. "I was just leaving."

Callie stepped in front of him, blocking his path. "What are you hiding?"

He stood a moment as if he were going to defy her, then sheepishly pulled his hand from behind his back, revealing a brown paper bag.

"Your dinner?" Callie asked pointedly.

Hank shuffled his feet and his face turned beet red. "Nah." He opened the sack and held it for her inspection. "We caught ourselves a mouse."

Callie threw a hand up, blocking her view. "No, please. I don't need to see." A shudder shook her shoulders, and she laughed weakly at her own foolishness. "Sorry, Hank."

"That's okay." He wadded the top of the sack closed in his fist. "What are you doing up here at this hour?"

"I went to the Blue Bell to see Judd."

"He's already gone home."

"Yes, I know. I was on my way back to the hotel—" She considered a moment telling Hank about the voice that had called out to her, then quickly discarded the idea. It had probably been the wind, and Hank more than likely already thought she had a screw or two loose from the way she'd acted a moment ago. "And I noticed the light up here and thought I'd left it on by mistake."

"Nah, it was me, checking the traps. I'm all done now, though, if you want me to walk you back to your hotel."

The hotel where Stephen possibly awaited her? Callie shook her head. "No. I think I'll stay here for a while."

"You'll be okay?"

She offered him a reassuring smile. "I'll be fine. But thanks."

Hank disappeared down the stairs. The outside door opened and closed. A blast of cold air crept up the stairway, making Callie aware of the already chilly temperature in the drafty old building.

She crossed to the sofa, rubbing her hands across her folded arms. Mary Elizabeth's diary still lay on the faded fabric where she'd left it the night before. Sighing, Callie picked it up, then pulled the chain to switch on the floor lamp by the sofa.

Memories of the previous night came rushing back. The eerie feeling of someone being upstairs with her. The lonely quality in the song Judd had played that had drawn her down to the bar. Finding him sitting on the stool, a guitar cradled against his chest. The kiss. The surge of passion. The warring emotions. The long, anticipatory walk back to the hotel. Being in Judd's arms. Making love.

She grabbed for the chain and pulled, throwing the room back into darkness. She didn't want lights. She wanted darkness to hide her troubled emotions.

She sagged onto the sofa, her chest tight, her throat burning with tears. Clutching the diary in one hand, she dragged the moth-eaten shawl she'd used the night before

across her chest. Tears budded and fell, rising in tempo and
intensity until her chest heaved with each gulp of air.

"Oh, Judd," she cried softly. "I need you."

"Callie?"

Callie tried to open her eyes, but her lids were simply too
heavy.

A hand touched hers and she stiffened at the unexpected
contact. She slowly relaxed as warmth and comfort stole
over her. Knowing somehow that there was nothing to fear
in the gesture, she curled her fingers around the offered
warmth and reassurance.

"Callie? Why are you crying?"

"I'm so confused."

"About what, dear?"

"Stephen."

"Your young man?"

"Yes. No." Callie swallowed back frustrated tears. "He's
not my young man. Everyone thinks he is, himself included, but he's not. He's just a friend."

"Is that the reason for your tears?"

"Partly, but the worst of it is that Stephen wants to marry
me."

"And you don't want to marry him?"

"No, but I don't want to hurt him, either. He's a dear
friend."

"That is a problem, for friends are too precious to lose."

"Yes, they are," Callie agreed, her heart heavy with the
weight of her problems, for she considered both Stephen
and Judd her friends. She reflected a moment on the feelings she felt for each of them. The first, a friendship
strengthened by years. The other, a passion that constantly
burned deeper and deeper. Her feelings for both were
strong.

"There is someone else," Callie murmured, testing the sound of the words as she shared them aloud for this first time.

"Oh?"

"Yes, which is crazy, because I've known him less than a week."

"And Stephen? How long have you known him?"

"Five years."

"And have your feelings for Stephen grown in that length of time?"

"No," Callie said slowly.

"Then perhaps time has nothing to do with feelings at all."

Callie tightened her fingers around the hand that held hers. "May I ask you a question?"

"Certainly, dear."

"How do you know when you're in love?"

A soft chuckle whispered over her. *"When you are in love, you won't have to ask that question. You will know."*

"But how?"

The hand on hers squeezed reassuringly. *"Your heart will tell you."*

Callie jerked to wakefulness, her heart thumping, her body drenched in a cold sweat. She pushed to an elbow and glanced around, sure that she wasn't alone.

Early morning rays kissed the main room of the whorehouse, its predawn glow masking the ravages of years of neglect. She dropped her head back on the pillow and groaned.

It was only a dream, she told herself, fighting back tears. Yet, already she yearned for the comfort she'd received from the mysterious woman in her dream, and the wisdom and strength of her words.

* * *

It was early yet, but Callie was anxious to get this over with. Taking a deep breath, she lifted her hand and knocked.

Stephen opened the door, fully dressed. "Good morning!" he said cheerfully.

Though he wore a smile, Callie saw the flicker of nervousness in his eyes at her unexpected appearance. She forced a smile in return. "Good morning, Stephen. Mind if I come in?"

He opened the door wide and motioned her inside. He watched her as she walked past. "I was waiting until I was sure you were up before I called to see if you would join me for breakfast."

"I've already eaten."

"Oh."

Unable to meet the disappointment in his eyes, Callie dropped her gaze. She knotted her hands at her waist and surged past him to cross to the window.

On the street below, Guthrie was showing signs of life. A merchant across the street was out sweeping the sidewalk in front of his store. An occasional car whizzed past. A lone jogger wearing fluorescent spandex and a stocking cap chugged out of sight.

The normalcy of their activities made Callie wish for some order in her own life. And she'd have that. The first step was setting things straight with Stephen. She struggled to find just the right words. "Stephen, this is difficult, but I hope you'll understand."

She turned to find him standing where she'd left him, watching her. "I know that you want to set a wedding date, but I—I can't."

"You need time," he said patiently.

"No. Time won't change my feelings. I simply can't marry you."

Stunned, he could only stare. "But, Callie, I love you."

His declaration of love had the desired effect. She felt herself weakening, hammered by guilt that she'd allowed their relationship to go on so long, then she stiffened, strengthening her resolve. She wouldn't, couldn't, let a sense of obligation keep her from doing what she knew was best for them both. "I love you, too, Stephen, but as a friend. Nothing more."

His eyes remained on her, his gaze unwavering. "You're sure?" he asked finally.

Callie bobbed her head, tears pushing at her throat. "Yes. I'm sure." She crossed quickly to him and rose to her toes to press a kiss on his cheek before heading for the door.

"Callie?"

She stopped with her hand on the knob. "Yes, Stephen?"

"If you change your mind..."

The offer hung between them, but Callie couldn't find the heart or the words to respond. Softly, she closed the door behind her.

Judd pulled the ball from his pocket and let it fly. Baby churned grass as he raced after the yellow fluorescent orb. Usually the game brought a smile to Judd. But not today. His heart hurt too bad. He sighed and dropped back against the cold marble monument behind him as he rubbed a hand across his chest as if he could ease the pain.

He stole a glance down the street to the Harrison House, his eyes instinctively seeking Callie's second-floor room. The shade was down, the drapes drawn. He wondered if she still slept. He wondered, too, if Stephen slept with her. The same bed that he and Callie had shared the night before. The thought made him squeeze his eyes tightly shut to block the the image.

Baby raced back with the ball and dropped it at Judd's feet. When Judd didn't pick it up, the dog stuck his nose against Judd's hand and nudged.

Judd gave him a half-hearted scratch behind the ears. "Sorry, Baby. I'm not much in the mood to play today." He scooped the ball from the ground and stood, shoving it deep into his duster pocket. "Let's take a walk." With a slap on his thigh, he signaled Baby to follow. Together they headed off down the street.

They'd almost reached the corner of First and Harrison when Judd saw him. Stephen. Callie's fiancé. Stepping out of the entrance to the Harrison Hotel. The expression he wore wasn't what Judd would expect to see on the face of a man who'd just spent the night with his fiancée. His shoulders were tense, his mouth set in a grim line. He crossed to the sleek silver car with the Texas license plates and tossed a leather garment bag into the trunk.

Was he leaving? So soon?

Judd didn't want to see the man, much less feel obligated to speak. Justified or not, the feelings were honest. He started to cross the street to avoid him, but he was too late. Stephen saw him and lifted a hand in greeting.

"Good morning, Judd."

Judd's greeting was a little more reserved. "Mornin'." He drew even with the car and cut a glance to the open trunk and the suitcase inside. "Thought you were staying the weekend."

Stephen's mouth twisted in a sardonic smile as he slammed the trunk lid. "So did I, but things didn't work out as I'd hoped." He rubbed his hands briskly together and hunched his shoulders against the cold. He stuck out his hand and forced a smile. "It was nice meeting you. If you're ever performing in Dallas, let me know. I'll try to catch one of your concerts."

Judd didn't bother to tell him he wasn't doing concerts anymore, but shook the offered hand. "Yeah, sure thing." After all, it wasn't Stephen's fault he'd gotten himself engaged to a liar.

* * *

"Let me make sure I understand all this. You think the grave out at Summit View Cemetery that bears the name William Leighton Sawyer, does *not* contain the body of William Leighton Sawyer?"

"That's correct."

"Then whose body do you think is in the grave?"

"I don't know. Possibly no one."

"And what proof do you have that the body of William Leighton Sawyer doesn't rest in that grave?"

Callie pulled out the birth certificate and leaned to lay it on the desk in front of the lawyer. "This is my great-grandfather's birth certificate. He is very much alive and lives in Dallas, Texas."

The lawyer shoved his glasses back on his nose and lifted his chin to peer through the bifocals at the document in front of him. He studied it, turning it over, then holding it up to the light. "Looks authentic to me," he muttered.

"I assure you it is." Callie settled back in the chair. "What legal action is necessary in order to exhume the grave?"

The lawyer reared back and pursed his lips, studying Callie over the top of his glasses. "You're sure you want to do this?"

"Positive."

The chair squeaked as he lowered it back into position and took up a pen. "I'll have to draw up the Exhumation Order and file it with the District Court Judge. You'll have to sign the papers as primary next of kin."

"Primary next of kin?"

He looked up from his note taking. "You are the closest living relative, aren't you?"

"No, not exactly."

He laid down his pen. "Who is?"

"Both of his children are deceased, so I suppose my mother is, since she's the oldest grandchild."

"Then she'll need to sign the order. There will be expenses involved."

Callie stood, her hopes sagging. There was no way in hell Frances Sawyer Benson would go to the expense of paying a lawyer and having a grave exhumed to satisfy an old man's whim. But she knew she couldn't give up until she'd at least tried to convince her. "Thank you for your time," she told the lawyer. "I'll let you know what my mother wishes to do."

Callie squeezed her temples with one hand while keeping the phone pressed to her ear with the other.

"I'm not asking you to rob a grave, Mother. I'm simply asking you as Papa's closest living relative to sign the Exhumation Order."

"Whether I dig it up myself or order it done, the result is the same. The grave is robbed."

"We are not robbing the grave! We simply want to prove that William Leighton Sawyer is not in the grave."

"We already know that, so what's the point?"

Worn out from arguing with her mother, Callie dipped her head to her palm. "The point is, there is a grave here with Papa's name on it. I want to know why. Don't you?"

"No," she said simply. "And besides, there are bound to be expenses involved. Who will bear the brunt of these costs?"

"I will."

"And my signature is required before any of this can transpire?"

"Yes."

Silence hummed for a good five seconds. Callie waited, not daring to breathe, much less hope.

"Have you spoken to Stephen?"

The abrupt change of topic took Callie by surprise. "Yes. He drove up yesterday."

"Is he still there?"

"No, he left for Dallas this morning."

"Obviously, he wasn't able to persuade you to forget this nonsense about locating Papa's mother."

"No, he wasn't."

"Did the two of you make up and set a wedding date?"

"It's not a matter of making up, Mother."

In exasperation, her mother cried, "Then why won't you set a date and marry him, for God's sake, and do something sensible with your life for a change?"

"Because I don't love him enough to marry him."

"Love," Frances flung back at her. "You and your silly concept about love. Friendship is what's important. And respect. The rest will take care of itself."

"Not for me, Mother."

Callie could hear the swell of anger before her mother replied, "Well, you might as well pack your things and come home, because I'm not signing any Exhumation Order."

"I'm not coming home, Mother. With or without your help, I intend to find out everything I can about Papa's mother."

With the appointment with the lawyer behind her and still feeling the effect of the call to her mother, Callie headed down the sidewalk toward the Blue Bell. She hadn't allowed herself to think about her confrontation with Judd. She couldn't. Not when she had the appointment with the lawyer and her mother to deal with. But now that her obligations were complete, her thoughts turned to Judd, and Stephen's ill-timed introduction of her at the Sand Plum the night before.

This is the young woman I was telling you about earlier, my fiancée, Callie Benson.

She shuddered at the memory of Judd's face. He'd immediately become the gunslinger again, the lines around his mouth and eyes hard and unforgiving. He'd swung his gaze briefly her way, giving her no more notice than he would a stranger. But she'd seen the hurt, the betrayal in his eyes before he'd turned away.

She approached the Blue Bell, her nerves jumping beneath her skin, and opened the door to find Hank standing behind the bar.

Callie forced a smile. "Catch any mice this morning?"

Hank laughed good-naturedly. "Nah. Maybe tonight, though."

Callie glanced around. "Is Judd here?"

"No, he hasn't been in yet. Expect him before long, though."

"Oh." Callie tried to hide her disappointment. "Well, I'll be working upstairs. When he comes in, would you tell him I need to talk to him?"

"Sure thing."

Callie climbed the staircase that led from the bar to the second floor, her spirits sagging. She wasn't sure how much longer her nerves could take the suspense.

Less than an hour later, she heard his steps. She rushed from her studio, then stopped midway across the main room, her heart sinking at her first glimpse of him.

His walk was almost a swagger, his face set in the hard lines she'd learned to dread. She could feel the anger emanating from him, almost taste it in the thick, musty air. He held the frown in place as he shortened the distance between them. "Hank said you needed to talk to me," he said curtly.

Callie tried to smile. "Yes, I do. About—about Stephen."

"Seemed like a nice guy," he said through tight lips.

"He is a nice guy."

He cocked a hip to one side and gave the brim of his Stetson an impatient punch with a finger. "Listen, if you're worried about what happened the other night, don't be. That'll be our little secret." Before Callie could respond, he added, "It was a roll in the hay, was all. A one-night stand. Don't lose any sleep over it. I assure you, I won't."

Callie sucked in a shocked breath. "That's all it was to you? A roll in the hay?"

His lips curved in a lazy grin. "Why sure, honey." He raised his thumb to line her lower lip, the action as provocative as it was demeaning. "Ain't nothin' wrong with a little cheat between friends." He dropped his hand and winked. "Anytime you feel like another roll, you give me a call, you hear?"

Seven

A roll in the hay. A little cheat between friends.

Judd's words burned in Callie's chest like a physical pain, searing the scar he'd left on her heart. She told herself it didn't matter, that she didn't care, it had been the same for her.

But it was a lie. Not an hour passed that she didn't think of him, wish for him.

Sleep became her enemy, her dreams filled with Judd. She would awaken with tears dampening her pillow and her heart heavy with memories she'd rather forget. With nothing but her work to console her, she mired herself in her project, working twelve, sometimes sixteen hour days. The statue grew, both in height and emotion, yet the face of the woman continued to elude Callie. She lacked focus, she told herself, and tried to blank out the nagging memories of Judd.

But his words continued to haunt her.

A roll in the hay. A little cheat between friends.

God, how could she have been such a fool! She never wanted to feel that level of pain again. Never.

For over a week Callie's presence in the building wore on Judd's nerves like the irritating drip of a leaky faucet. He heard her when she unlocked the door of a morning and creaked her way up the stairs. He heard her gentle rustlings as she moved about above him throughout the day. Most nights he was still in the bar when she creaked her way back down the stairs and let herself out the side door. She never once approached him or acknowledged him in any way. Stubbornness born of pride kept him from approaching her.

But after a week neither pride nor stubbornness could keep him from going upstairs after she'd left, to see what she found to do up there all day.

He waited until the bar was closed for the night and Hank had polished the last glass and gone home. Left alone with his curiosity, he took a flashlight from behind the bar and trudged his way up the stairs. He crossed to the room Callie used as her studio and flipped on the light. Unlike the rest of the second story, the floor of this room was swept clean. A table sat in the center of the room, and a plastic-covered, odd-shaped mound rested on its top.

A stool stood next to the table and across it was thrown a stained smock. Knowing she'd worn it only moments before, Judd picked up the smock and lifted it to his face, absorbing the warmth of her body that still clung to it. He inhaled deeply, savoring her scent. Wildflowers. Always wildflowers.

His fingers curled into the stained cloth as his heart cried out for her. To see her, touch her, hold her.... Angrily, he tossed the smock aside. She'd deceived him, he told himself. She belonged to another man, never to him.

Wanting to accomplish his purpose in coming upstairs and then escape the painful reminders, he lifted a corner of the plastic. He could see just enough of the exposed statue to whet his curiosity. Careful not to damage anything, he slowly lifted off the cover. His breath came out in an admiring whistle as a woman's bare legs came into view, every toe, muscle and tendon molded in perfect symmetry.

He lifted the cloth higher to find an infant cradled in the woman's arms, suckling a breast. Each detail was so lifelike that he swore he saw veins bulge on the swollen breast at the infant's gentle prodding. He tossed the cloth aside to see the woman's forehead tipped toward that of the infant. He dipped his knees to better see her face and sucked in a raw, startled breath.

He laid a finger against the cold clay where the woman's face should be. He moved his finger slowly, carefully, feeling a slight indentation where the eyes should be and a hint of a swell where a nose and mouth should be. Everything else was blank. Cold. Smooth. No facial features, no expression. It was almost spooky.

"What do you think you are doing?"

Judd jerked his hand away and whirled to find Callie, her arms folded tightly across her breasts, standing in the doorway. She looked like a ghost, her face pale, her features gaunt, dark circles beneath her eyes. But the pull he felt toward her told him she was no apparition.

"I thought you left," he said, neatly sidestepping her question.

She crossed and scooped a key from the corner of the table. "I did, but halfway to the hotel I realized I'd forgotten my room key." She rammed the key in her jacket pocket and turned an accusing look on Judd. "Now that we've ascertained the purpose of my presence, what are *you* doing here?"

He nodded toward the statue. "I was looking at your work."

Callie caught the plastic drape in her hands and swept it up and over the statue. "To make sure I was a sculptress?"

she said, her voice heavy with sarcasm. "Did you think I deceived you about that, too?"

"No."

"Then why are you here?"

"Curiosity. I wanted to see what you do all day up here."

"I work."

He nodded toward the now-shrouded figures. "I can see that. It's going to be something when you're finished."

"If I finish it."

"You mean when you finish it."

Her anger at Judd grew to encompass her frustration at her inability to finish the project. "No, I mean *if*."

"But all you lack is the face."

Callie sank down on the stool and dropped her face to her hands. "I can't sculpt it," she mumbled against her fingers. "I just can't do it."

She looked so miserable, so defeated sitting there, Judd was tempted to gather her up in his arms and comfort her. Before he could act on the impulse, she snapped up her head. She stared hard at the plastic, the features on her own face tightening. "I can see it up here," she said, giving the center of her forehead a thump with the heels of her palms. "But for some reason," she said, lowering her hands to glare at them in disgust, "I can't translate those images onto the clay."

"Maybe you're trying too hard."

"Yeah, right," she said dryly. She dropped her elbows to her knees and her chin in her palms. "I see it more as a continuation of the legacy."

Judd quirked an eyebrow her way. "Legacy?"

"Miss Lizzy's." When he continued to look at her in puzzlement, she felt obligated to explain. "The emotion I want to evoke is that of a new mother, looking at her infant for the first time. I want to capture the feelings she must be experiencing. The love, the pride, the awe,

"But every time I lay my hands on the clay," she said, her voice turning to a low growl, "I think of Lizzy and how she shipped her son off to Boston, never to see him again." She glared at the statue, a frown building between her eyes. "How could a mother do that to her own flesh and blood?"

"You don't know that she did."

Callie jerked her gaze to Judd's, her frown deepening.

He decided to change tactics. The mention of Lizzy always seemed to upset Callie, and she was upset enough as it was. "What about your own mother? Think about her instead."

"My mother?" Callie laughed, though the sound lacked mirth. "Envisioning her is almost as debilitating to my creativity as envisioning Miss Lizzy, although to her credit," she added reluctantly, "my mother didn't send me away."

"Oh, come on, she couldn't be that bad."

"Worse." But Callie didn't want to think about her mother. It only reminded her of their previous conversation and her anger at her mother's refusal to sign the Exhumation Order. Callie knew Frances was using the order as a power play. It wouldn't be the first time she'd held something over Callie's head in order to get her way. All Callie had to do was set a date to marry Stephen and her mother would sign the order. It was that simple.

Suddenly weary, she pushed to her feet. "Well, I'm going to head back to the hotel. Turn out the light when you leave."

"Wait, and I'll walk you."

Already at the door, Callie turned and looked at him, her face as void of emotion as the statue that haunted her. "Thanks, but I'm not interested in another 'roll in the hay.'"

He'd deserved the verbal slap, but knowing that didn't take the sting out of Callie's refusal. It grated on Judd as he prowled the Blue Bell long after she'd left.

Hell! he thought angrily. He hadn't offered her a roll in the hay. All he'd offered was to walk her back to her room.

He found himself standing on the postage-stamp-size stage, his guitar less than a foot away. Hoping to find comfort in his music as he had in the past, he picked up the instrument and sat down on the edge of the stage. He settled his arm in the familiar curve and strummed a few chords. He hummed a bar of the song he'd been working on, closed his eyes then let the music take him. The words flowed out of him easily, as if piped from his heart.

As the last note faded, he smiled with satisfaction, proud of the lyrics, the music. They were all his. Not that anybody would ever hear it but him.

But Callie had, he remembered. And she'd said it would be a hit.

He slapped the flat of his hand against the sounding board, sending a hollow keen reverberating through his hand. She had even invaded the one part of his life that had remained exclusively his, that he'd thought no one could take away. His music.

Heaving a frustrated sigh, he set the instrument aside. Until he talked with Callie, unloaded all the anger that knotted in his chest, he wasn't going to get her off his mind. And now was as good a time as any, he told himself as he pushed to his feet.

Yanking his duster from the rack by the entrance, he stormed out the door, slamming and locking it behind him. As he strode for the hotel, his eyes immediately sought her window. The shades were drawn, the drapes pulled. No light showed around the edges. She was probably asleep, he thought irritably, but that was too damn bad because she was about to have some company, whether she wanted it or not.

He strode through the hotel lobby and breathed a sigh of relief to see that Frank was away from the desk. He sure didn't want to have to explain his appearance at this hour of the night. Too impatient to wait on the elevator, he took the stairs, bolting up them two at a time. He reached her door, slightly breathless, but more from nerves than exertion.

He rapped lightly, waited, then knocked again a little louder. He heard the scrape of a light switch turning and her muffled, "Who's there?" He stood with his feet braced and his hands on his hips, knowing fully well that she was looking at him through the peephole in the door. Even though he couldn't see her, he stared right back, his mouth set in a determined line.

"Let me in, Callie."

"Let you in? Do you realize what time it is?"

"Yes, now open the door or I'll kick it down."

The dead bolt scraped, the knob twisted and Callie appeared, her blue eyes blazing. "What in the hell do you mean 'you'll kick it down'?" She flattened a hand against his chest and shoved. "Listen, buster, you may throw your weight around and get your way with other women, but that tough cowboy act doesn't work with me. As far as I'm concerned, you can take your ten-gallon hat and shove it up your—"

His hands clamped at her elbows and he dragged her up against him, crushing his mouth over hers. She tasted the anger on his lips; the heat of it scorched her throat and burned behind her eyes. Need was there, too, in every thrust of his tongue, every scrape of his teeth against hers.

Please don't do this to me, she cried inwardly. *Please don't make me want you.* With her hands trapped between them, she pressed for distance, if not physical then at least an emotional one. His hands tightened on her elbows at the resistance, but his mouth gentled on hers, leaving her helpless, her breasts heaving against his chest. He nipped lightly at her lower lip, then flicked his tongue seductively at the upper bow. "Tell me you don't want this," he demanded, his voice husky with need.

"I don't."

"Liar," he whispered, catching the back of her head in his hand. Her lips parted beneath the pressure of his tongue, and he swallowed her groan of submission. His mouth moved over hers, demanding answers to questions unasked, taking pleasure in the slow melting of her body against his, punishing her because she belonged to another man.

Leaning back, he caught her face roughly in his hands. "Why, Callie? Why didn't you tell me about Stephen?"

Her face tipped up to his, her eyes heavy, her lips swollen. She whispered back, "There was nothing to tell."

His hands tightened on her cheeks. "A fiancé? I'd think you might have mentioned it."

Angered, Callie twisted from his grasp. "He is *not* my fiancé."

It took a minute for her words to register and when they did, Judd could only stare. As far as he could determine, that only left one explanation. "You broke it off, then?"

"There was nothing to break off."

"But—"

"Stephen assumed we would marry," she cried in frustration. "There was never a proposal, a ring, a date set. He just assumed.... And I never had the heart to tell him otherwise." The events of the past week caught up with her—the emotional confrontation with Stephen, Judd's heartbreaking rejection. Tears budding, she whirled for her room. She caught the edge of the door in her hand and gave it a hard push to close it behind her.

Judd braced a palm against it to keep it from slamming in his face. His eyes on her back, he closed the door behind them.

"So you're not engaged," he finally said.

Callie rubbed her hands up and down her crossed arms as if chilled. "No."

"And Stephen? Does he know how you feel?"

"Yes."

He knew by her posture that it hadn't been easy for her. He'd found himself in similar situations when a woman would think there was more between them than a good time. Even though he'd let them down as gently as he could, there were usually hurt feelings and a friendship lost. Judd remembered the look on Stephen's face when he'd seen him loading his suitcase in his car and knew that Callie had probably lost a friend.

Because he understood how Callie felt, he touched her elbow. "I'm sorry. I didn't know."

A shudder shook her, but she refused to cry. She lifted her chin and continued to look straight ahead. "Apology accepted. Now if you don't mind, I'd like for you to leave."

"No." His hand still at her elbow, he took a step closer, taking her other elbow in hand as well. He molded his body to hers and buried his nose in her hair. The unmistakable scent of wildflowers curled around him.

A sob built in Callie's throat as she fought the desire to turn in his arms. "I already told you, Judd, I don't want another roll in the hay."

Regret for the callous words he'd thrown at her wrung his heart. Groaning, he skimmed his hands down her forearms to circle her waist and gathered her to him. He dropped his chin to her shoulder and his mouth next to her ear. "It was never that, Callie. Not for me."

She tried hard to ignore the warmth of his breath, the tenderness of his touch, the strength and comfort of his arms around her. But her heart wouldn't allow it. The love she felt for him, the pain when he'd told her their night together meant nothing, twisted in her heart, reopening the wound. She spun in his arms, her cheeks wet with tears. "But you said—"

He caught her to him, burying his face against the side of her neck as he wound his arms around her, not wanting to hear his own words repeated again. "I didn't mean it. I swear I didn't. I—I'm sorry. I was angry and I wanted to hurt you like you hurt me. But I didn't mean it, I swear I didn't."

Her body remained stiff and unyielding. He knew that his careless words had cut deeply and knew, too, that if she chose not to forgive him this time, he wouldn't blame her. The decision was hers to make. He stepped from her, letting his arms slowly fall to his sides. "If you still want me to leave, I will."

Her breath hitched once, then twice as she looked at him through tear-filled eyes. "Don't you dare," she whispered.

Her response was so unexpected it took a second for Judd to realize what she'd said. When he did, he grabbed her to him so tight the breath squeezed from her lungs.

"I never knew love could hurt this much," he said, his voice breaking slightly at the admission.

"Oh, Judd," Callie whispered back. She sank her fingers in the dark hair that curled at his neck and drew his face to hers. "Neither did I."

It was the most beautiful time of day in Judd's estimation, those quiet, dark hours just before dawn. He'd seen it from both sides—drawing a shade against it as he crawled into bed exhausted after a long concert or waking up on his bus to peer out the darkened window at an ever-changing highway on the road to a new town, a new show. He'd grown to appreciate the solitude and beauty of this particular time of day, but nothing matched the beauty of this one.

Silently, he watched Callie, standing before the window, naked as the day she was born, one hand caught in the drape. Her hair was mussed, her lips swollen from the pressure of his own. Her eyes had a faraway look that made him wonder what thoughts were going through her head.

Unable to resist, he swung from the bed and crossed to her, gathering her lightly in his arms. He dipped his mouth to her shoulder and nipped. "Couldn't you sleep?"

She crossed her arms over his and relaxed against him, letting his chest take her weight. "No."

"Penny for your thoughts."

She laughed softly, her gaze still on that faraway something beyond the window. "They aren't even worth that much." Sighing, she laid her head against his cheek, a worry wrinkle forming between her eyes.

Judd turned her in his arms. "Hey. What's this?" he asked, rubbing the ball of his thumb against the crease. "Regrets?"

Callie caught his hand in hers and pressed her lips to his palm to reassure him. "No," she said, smiling up at him. "No regrets." She turned her gaze on the window again. "It's the statue. I can't get it off my mind."

"If it bothers you that much, call and cancel. Tell them you can't get it done on time."

Callie shook her head. "No. I've never failed to deliver a commissioned piece on schedule."

Judd understood and respected that sense of responsibility. There were times on the road when he would've loved to cancel a show and go home. But he never had. "Is there anything I can do to help?"

"Short of making Miss Lizzy the model mother?" Callie laughed and hugged him to her. "No, there's nothing you can do." She gave him a peck on the cheek and turned from his embrace.

Frowning, Judd watched her walk away. "Maybe I *can* help."

Callie looked at him, her forehead knitted. "How?"

"Have you got time for a little walk?"

Callie looked at him curiously. "I suppose."

Judd picked up a pair of sweats from the chair and tossed them to her, then reached for his own jeans.

Once outside the hotel, he caught her elbow, guiding her down the brick sidewalk. At the entrance to the alley just behind the building housing the saloon, he stopped. Releasing her arm, he lifted his hand and pointed upward. "See that square of brick up there that looks a little newer than the rest?"

Callie squinted into the darkness, searching the wall until she found the square she thought he indicated. "Yes, I see it."

He waved his hand, taking in the building that stood opposite the Blue Bell. "That used to be the Elks Hotel. A catwalk used to join the two buildings," he explained as he slowly drew an imaginary line through the air until his finger pointed at the building the Blue Bell was housed in. Callie saw a similar square of newer brick where he pointed. "Men would register at the hotel, travel across the catwalk and visit the whorehouse and their activities would never be known."

He caught her elbow and guided her around the corner to the door of the whorehouse. Digging in his pocket, he pulled out a ring of keys, selected one and unlocked the door. "Some used this entrance, but not as many as used the catwalk." He gestured Callie in, then closed the door. Darkness swallowed them. Not at all sure what this was about, Callie folded her arms across her breasts and rubbed at the goose bumps that had popped up.

The wheel of a cigarette lighter grated in the silence followed by the flicker of a small flame. Judd brushed past her as he stepped to the stairwell and hit a light switch. The single light bulb at the top of the stairs popped on, throwing a ladder of light on the weathered steps. He took the steps slowly, talking. "About nine or ten women lived here at a time. The stories are that the women in this house were the cleanest, most respectable whores in the territory." His foot hit the top step and he paused, waiting for Callie to catch up. He gestured to the main room. "This was the parlor where the girls entertained the men until they sought the privacy of their rooms.

"Their clients were, for the most part, wealthy and influential men. Government officials, investors and drummers came here on business and usually stayed at the hotel. They'd sneak across the catwalk, visit a while with the girls, then head down that staircase," he said, indicating the second staircase on the far side of the room that led to the bar. "They'd have a couple of drinks in the Blue Bell, then cross the street to a gaming hall, using the underground tunnel. For the most part, the citizens of Guthrie were never the wiser."

"This is all very fascinating, but what is your point?"

Judd ducked his head and stuffed his hands deep into his jeans pockets. "Lizzy Sawyer was the madam."

Callie's chin dropped and her arms fell limply to her sides. "What did you say?"

"I said she was the madam. You do know what a madam is, don't you?"

"Y-yes, of course I do." Shock gradually gave way to anger. "Why didn't you tell me this before now?"

"I didn't think it was necessary. Your opinion of the woman was already pretty low."

"And it appears that I was right," she said, folding her arms at her breasts. "Mary Elizabeth Sawyer was exactly what her family claimed she was, a spoiled woman who thought only of her own selfish wants and needs." She unfolded her arms and lifted her hands to cover her mouth as her thoughts raced ahead to the effect this would have on her great-grandfather. "Poor Papa," she murmured against her fingertips. "I can't imagine how upsetting this will be for him."

"She wasn't a bad woman, Callie."

Callie wheeled to stare at him. "Not bad? For God's sake," she cried, tossing her hands in the air. "She was the madam of a whorehouse, shipped her own son off to be raised by his grandparents, whom, by her own admission, she detested. And you say she wasn't bad?"

"I don't know anything about how she became known as the madam of the whorehouse, or what transpired with her son. But I do know a little about her." He caught her hand and dragged her to a window. "See that church over there, the one whose steeple is peeking up over the trees?"

"Yes."

"Miss Lizzy worshiped there every Sunday. In the early years of the settlement, times were hard. There were droughts, sickness and crop failures. Miss Lizzy cared for those who couldn't care for themselves. She nursed them and provided food. During the depression she started a clothes closet to serve the needs of the community. She provided supplies and helped cook and served meals to those who wouldn't have eaten otherwise." He took her shoulders and turned her slightly, angling her a little to the left. "And that building over there? See it? That's the old library. There's a new one now, and the old building has been turned into a museum, but the original library was kept open partially by the generous donations of Lizzy Bodean."

Callie pressed her hands over her ears, unwilling to hear anymore. "Stop it!" she cried. "I don't want to hear this."

Judd dropped his arms from her shoulders. "No, I guess you probably don't." He crossed to an old trunk, one that Callie hadn't found the time to dig through yet. He lifted the lid and poked around a bit, then lifted out a book. He crossed back to Callie, extending it to her.

She doubled her hands into a single fist at her waist, refusing to take it. "What is that?" she asked, her eyes riveted to the faded leather volume.

"Miss Lizzy's journal of her journey to the Oklahoma Territory and her first year here." He prodded her hand with the book, forcing her to accept it. "You might want to read it."

Her gaze flicked to his. "Why?"

"It might help you understand her more." He stepped back, knowing he'd done all he could to remove the ill feelings she held for her great-great-grandmother, the woman whose legacy threatened to rob her of her creativity. The rest would be left up to Miss Lizzy and the power of her words... and the story she had to tell.

Callie tossed the book to the table and dragged the plastic from her statue. She didn't need to read the journal to know what kind of woman Lizzy Sawyer was. She was selfish and cold-blooded, just like the rest of her family. So what if the woman spread a little of her wealth around? She'd probably done those good deeds to ease her guilt over abandoning her son.

Sniffing, she sank down on the stool and picked up a sculpting knife. She gently rolled it back and forth, warming the wooden handle between her palms, while she stared at the blank face before her. She didn't have time for thoughts of Lizzy Sawyer Bodean. She had work to do.

Carefully and methodically, she emptied her mind of thoughts of her sordid relative. She closed her eyes, willing the emotions she needed to the surface.

Slowly they washed over her and the image appeared behind her closed lids. A mother. Gentle, loving. Holding her baby for the first time. Emotions pushing at the young mother's throat, gathering behind her eyes as she marveled at the miracle before her. A part of herself, created in love, nourished by hope. Born of strength and determination.

Callie slowly opened her eyes, the emotions fresh, the sculpting knife warm in her hand. She lifted the tool, her eyes unfocused, still seeing the mother's face in her mind. She shifted on the stool, bringing the knife and the image to the clay. Her hand stopped an inch short of the statue, as if grasped by a hand from behind. She strained against it, fighting to hold on to the emotions, needing to sculpt that image before it was lost . . . but her hand slammed to the table. The knife shot from her grip, cartwheeled across the table and fell to clatter against the hardwood floor.

Dropping her head to her hands, Callie heaved a deep, shuddery breath and gave in to the anger. Hot tears streaked down her face while she funneled her fingers through her hair.

Callie, dear, don't cry.

Callie snapped up her head, her heart thudding at the sound of the familiar voice. "Who are you?" she whispered, her voice tinged with fear. Her question echoed hollowly in the empty room. Slowly she spun on the stool, dragging her fingertips beneath her eyes to clear them, but saw nothing but the cracks in the walls and the cobwebs draping the corners.

"Please," Callie begged, her voice thick with frustrated tears. "Tell me who you are, what you want from me."

The voice came again, this time from behind her.

I want nothing, only to give. Read the journal. Perhaps then you'll understand.

Callie whirled to find the doorway behind her empty.

The leather spine cracked and popped like an old woman's knees as Callie laid open the book. The handwriting was familiar, the same flourishes and sweeps of the diary she'd read earlier.

Scowling, she settled into a corner of the tattered sofa and began to read.

January 3, 1890:

I cannot believe I found the courage to do it! My heart races at the very thought! Sneaking out the window, sliding down the roof, the frightening climb from the branches of the elm tree . . . and Ethan, my love, my champion, waiting in the shadows beneath it.

Callie's fingers tightened on the book's faded leather covers as she realized the stories Papa had told her about his mother running off with a man to the Oklahoma Territory were true. She swallowed back the sense of dread and made herself read on.

January 15, 1890:
Ethan worries so about my safety and my health, although I assure him I feel fine. He even suggested I return home, promising to send for me later. But the birth of our child is months away, and I am sure we'll reach the Oklahoma Territory in ample time to prepare for the arrival.

She was pregnant when she left home! Anxious to find the details of Papa's birth, Callie flipped pages, skimming ahead.

February 19, 1890:
I try very hard not to worry, but I am afraid I fail miserably at the task. Ethan assures me that when we reach St. Louis, he will send a wire to his bank and request they transfer his funds to him there. In the meantime, my reticule grows lighter and lighter.

He's using her for her money, Callie thought with a stab of anger. No wonder her parents didn't approve of Ethan. She'd fallen in love with the lowest form of man...a gigolo.

March 20, 1890:
My heart feels unusually heavy today, for I had to sell Mother's pearls. They were given to Mother on her sixteenth birthday and in turn she gave them to me on mine. I had always thought I would pass them down to

my daughter. But I must not think such forlorn thoughts! I am here, traveling across the country with the man I love. And Ethan has promised to buy me a hundred strings of pearls to replace the ones we sold. That is what I shall focus on. A gift from Ethan. A string of pearls. If I close my eyes, I can almost feel the weight of them around my neck.

April 23, 1890:
Almost three months have passed since we first left Boston. I sometimes wonder about my family, what they are doing, whether or not they miss me. Silly thoughts, really, for I know that when I left, they closed the book on my life, just as they threatened if I persisted in seeing Ethan.

The train ride, though thrilling, is grueling on my back. I suppose it is all the sitting required of me. As I pen this, Ethan is in the lounge playing a game of cards with some gentlemen he met earlier. I wish I were there with him. Anything to escape this suffocating car with the windows blowing cinders in my face.

Angered by the woman's blind loyalty to a man not worth the ground she walked on, Callie flipped pages.

June 9, 1890:
Ethan's absence is distressing, at best. I cannot bear to think what might have delayed him. Mrs. Grindel continues to look at me with suspicion, always inquiring about Ethan's return. Oh, Ethan, please come soon and take me away from this horrid house.

June 14, 1890:
I'm writing by lamplight, which I'm sure Mrs. Grindel will complain about tomorrow when she discovers the oil is low. I cannot sleep for the pain keeps me awake.

My back again, lower and much more intense than ever before. I am so frightened! I fear the baby will come before Ethan's return. If so, who will assist at the birth? With whom shall I share the glorious arrival of the birth of our child?

June 17, 1890:
My heart is shredded into a thousand pieces. Our child is dead. A son. Ethan would have been so proud to have a son carry on his name. Mrs. Grindel and her sister Lucinda attended the birth. They said the cord was wrapped around his neck and there was nothing they could do to save him. My heart grieves for him, for I never even saw his face or held him in my arms. Mr. Grindel buried him properly and has promised to take me to his grave as soon as I'm able to travel.

Writing is difficult, for my hand shakes uncontrollably and my head swims in confusion. The medicine Mrs. Grindel gives me makes me sleep and dulls my thoughts. Oh, Ethan, please come soon. I need you so. How will I ever find the strength to tell you our son is gone from us?

Callie closed the book and dropped it to the floor, tears streaming down her face. Lizzy hadn't sent her child away. She'd really thought he'd died. She'd loved him, grieved for him... and she'd done it alone, without her precious Ethan or her parents' comfort and support.

Standing, she swiped the tears from her cheeks and crossed to her workroom. She bent to pick up the knife from the floor, then scooted the stool close to the table and sat before the figure. With her eyes flooded with tears, her heart filled with the emotions transported through time by words, she lifted the sculpting knife.

* * *

Judd closed the door behind the last customer, twisted the dead bolt in place, then turned and ran for the stairs, taking them two at a time.

He'd given Callie the time alone he'd thought she needed. He'd worked all day with one ear tuned to the noises upstairs. He'd heard the reluctant scrape of her shoes on the floor overhead and the squeak of cushions when she'd flopped down on the old sofa. He'd suspected she'd given in enough to at least read the book. For hours he'd paced, listening, waiting on customers, making himself stay away. He'd heard the book hit the floor, and the first strangled sob. He was almost to the foot of the stairs when he'd heard the hurried patter of her shoes as she crossed back overhead to her workroom.

Stopping with his hand on the worn bannister, he had turned back to the bar and his customers, knowing he had to give her the time and the privacy to conquer her demons herself.

But now the bar was closed, the customers gone, and it had been hours since he'd heard a peep from upstairs. He had to check on her, see that she was all right.

He hit the top step running, then slowed to cross quietly to the far corner where her workroom was situated. The light was on, its rays spinning to silver the fine coat of dust on the main room's floor. He saw her through the open doorway, her rear end jutting off the stool, her heels hooked over the rung. One arm pillowed her head on the table, while her hand limply held a knife.

He tiptoed closer and peeked over her shoulder to find her eyes closed. He eased the knife from her hand, laid it aside and stooped, intending to pick her up. But then he saw it. The statue's face. The sight of it stole the breath from his lungs and the strength from his knees. He sagged against the table, flattening his hands on its top to support himself, his eyes riveted on the mesmerizing face.

The eyes were soft, full of warmth and love, and carried the sheen of unshed tears. The lips curved slightly in the barest hint of a smile as she looked down upon the babe in her arms, her eyes filled with a mixture of wonder and love. A tender finger lay gently on the cheek of the babe suckling at her breast.

Sweetness. Gentleness. Femininity. All woven together with an inner strength and pride. Callie had accomplished all she'd hoped for and more.

Turning to her, Judd scraped back a feathering of hair from her face and pressed a kiss on her cheek. Bending close, he eased her into his arms. She complained only slightly as he lifted her to his chest, but then she wound her arms around his neck, turned her cheek against his and nestled close.

His heart pounding with his love for the woman in his arms, he hit the light switch with his elbow, throwing the room into darkness.

Bless you both.

Judd stopped and glanced back. Moonlight streaked through the window, spotlighting the statue of the mother and her babe in its heavenly glow. A slow smile curled one corner of his lips as he whispered in return, "And bless you, Miss Lizzy."

Eight

Callie didn't stir again until Judd attempted to lay her on the bed in her hotel room, then it was only to tighten her arms around his neck when he started to withdraw. Touched by her unconscious need for him, he sank a knee into the cushiony mattress and laid down beside her, gathering her close to his heart.

She slept while he kept watch.

Hours later when she awakened, his gaze was still on her. She never questioned his presence in her bed or how she'd arrived there. The fact that he was there with her was enough. She smiled sleepily up at him. "I did it," she murmured.

Because he was an artist of sorts, he understood the satisfaction in that accomplishment. He squeezed her against him. "I know. I saw."

"I couldn't have done it without your help. Thank you."

"Miss Lizzy is the one to thank."

Callie smiled wistfully, remembering. "Yes, but without your insistence, I wouldn't have read her journal and discovered the truth."

Sure that she'd found something in the book he'd missed when he'd read it over a year ago, Judd lifted his head. "The truth? You mean about the grave?"

"No. I'll probably never know that. But I discovered something more important. Mary Elizabeth Sawyer wasn't the person her family portrayed her to be. I found her to be loving and generous to a fault. And I truly believe that she thought her son died at birth. When she wrote of it, I felt her grief as strongly as if it were my own."

"So the mystery is solved?"

"For me it is. So much time has passed that it really doesn't matter why Papa was sent away to Boston. What matters is that his mother didn't do the sending."

Her satisfaction in resolving the mystery surrounding her great-grandfather's mother was obvious. Although Judd wanted to share her happiness, he couldn't, for with the resolution came an end to her reason for remaining in Guthrie. "I guess you'll be going back to Dallas, then," he said quietly.

Callie tipped her face up to his and saw the trace of uncertainty in his eyes. Theirs was a tremulous relationship, based more on emotion than time, both reluctant to voice their feelings, unsure whether they were offering too much too soon. Wanting to ease his uncertainties—and in doing so, hopefully a few of her own by buying more time with him—she laid a fingertip against his lips. "Tracing my great-great-grandmother's past wasn't the only reason I came to Guthrie," she said helpfully.

His lips curved beneath her finger in the beginnings of a smile. His gaze on hers, he caught her finger between his teeth. "Why else did you come?" he asked, then closed his lips around the slender appendage and drew it deep into his mouth.

The sensation was so seductive, Callie could barely breathe much less think. "A vacation," she murmured absently, her eyes riveted to his. "I needed a vacation."

Slowly, achingly, he drew her finger from between his lips. He released it with a soft, moist plop. "I don't think you've had much of a vacation, do you?" he asked, then let her hand fall limply to his chest.

Through heavy lids, Callie watched the tip of her finger disappear in the mat of dark hair there. "No," she replied, hypnotized by the sight. "I don't guess I have."

"Seems a shame, doesn't it?" he said. "To leave before you have a chance to see all the sights?"

"Yes," she replied, lifting her gaze to his. "It does."

"You have, what, two weeks before the presentation in Houston?"

"Yes. But there's Thanksgiving."

"Do you have plans?"

"No."

"Good, then you can finish out your vacation, spend Thanksgiving with my family. If you want, you can even stay out at my place."

"Your place?" she asked, startled by the offer.

"Yeah."

"And where is that?"

"In the country, about ten miles north of town."

Shivers of anticipation raced through her at the thought of spending two weeks alone with him in the country. "Any neighbors?" she asked, hoping she didn't sound too eager.

"None to speak of."

"Sounds lonely."

"If we're lucky."

She propped her elbow on her pillow and leaned her head against her palm. "I'm feeling lucky," she said, lowering her voice suggestively.

Grinning, Judd threw his arm around her waist and hauled her to him. "Me, too."

* * *

"Where are we going first?" Callie asked, her eyes as charged with excitement as a second grader out on a school holiday.

Judd couldn't help but laugh as he tossed her suitcase in the back of his truck. "I thought we'd ride the trolley, get the official tour, see what interests you, then take my truck and backtrack."

Callie slipped her hand in his. "Sounds like a winner."

Judd handed her up on the trolley, then followed her to a seat. The bell clanged and the trolley eased from the curb and into traffic. Callie immediately pressed her nose to the window and listened as the guide began his spiel. Judd settled back, stretching his legs out in the narrow aisle, and watched Callie watch Guthrie, convinced he had the better view.

The tour lasted forty-five minutes, and by the time Callie stepped off the trolley she had scribbled a page full of sights she wanted to revisit.

"What's your pleasure?" Judd asked after they'd climbed back into his truck.

She looked at her list, then turned a hopeful eye to Judd. "Everything?" she asked, timidly.

Chuckling, he shifted into gear. "Everything it is." He retraced the trolley's route, his first stop the Logan County Courthouse where three weeks before Callie had found the records of Miss Lizzy's marriage. He parked the truck opposite the building. "Guthrie was born in a single day, April 22, 1889, when the government officially opened the Territory to settlement. People came from all over to take part in the run. Farmers, businessmen, speculators and profiteers." He chuckled, then added, "And the occasional riffraff.

"Guthrie was established as the Territorial capitol. Everyone assumed that once Oklahoma became a state, the capitol would remain here. Land was set aside for the future site and later a building was constructed. Everything was going as planned until June 11, 1910." He leaned across the seat and nodded up at the courthouse. "On that night the state seal was stolen from this building and taken to Oklahoma City. It was a shock, both emotionally and financially, to the people here who had invested so much on the supposition that the capitol of Oklahoma would be in Guthrie. In many ways, the community never recovered."

Callie heard the pride in his voice as much as the regret. "You love it here, don't you?"

"It's home."

"No, it's more than that," she insisted.

He shrugged, then chuckled ruefully. "There was a time when I was younger that I considered Guthrie the armpit of America. Couldn't wait to get out of here. I wanted the big city and a chance at fame that Guthrie couldn't offer me. At twenty-one, I threw my guitar and what belongings I could call my own in the back of an old truck, headed for Nashville and never looked back."

He sat a moment, one arm hooked over the steering wheel, lost in the memories. "Funny," he said, voicing his thoughts aloud. "But during the trial, all I could think about was getting back here. Where I could walk down the street without people staring and whispering. Where my family and friends were. Where a man's word is as good as gold. That's what kept me going."

He shook his head to clear the melancholy thoughts. "Anyway, after the trial, I did come back. The folks here accepted me with no questions asked. They've respected my privacy, protected it like it was their own." His lips thinned in determination. "I owe the folks in this town a big debt. Some day I hope to repay them by giving them back what they lost."

"But how? You can't possibly change the site of the state capitol back to Guthrie."

He shifted into gear. "No, but I can give them back their pride."

Easing off the clutch, he drove on while Callie stared at his profile, wondering if he realized that he, too, had been stripped of his pride. Not by political shenanigans as Guthrie had been, but by false accusations and a public that thrived on whatever dirt the media fed them. She suspected it was that loss of pride that had brought him home to Guthrie and forced him to give up his music career.

"This area is known as Capitol Hill," he said, interrupting her thoughts.

Forcing herself to pay attention to what he was saying, she listened while Judd pointed to a block of land and a cluster of buildings. "And that was Government Acre, land set aside for the capitol building. The building covering the square is the world's largest Scottish Rite Masonic Temple. The temple was built back in the 1920s with a price tag of over two million dollars. It has a ballroom, reading salons and two theaters that they rent out to the public. In fact, the Historical Society is having a concert there next month to raise money for future renovations."

"Will you be singing?"

He shook his head and shifted into gear. "Nope," he replied as he pulled away. "I don't sing anymore."

She felt his withdrawal as strongly as she felt the beat of her heart. And he was lying. He did sing. Maybe not for the public, but she'd heard him singing down in the Blue Bell when he'd thought he was alone. To confront him would be useless. She could see that.

He traversed residential and business streets alike, elaborating on the information the tour guide had shared. By the time they neared the old Masonic Children's Home, she was once again caught up in the history of Guthrie and stretched out a hand, motioning for him to stop.

Judd eased to the curb opposite the group of buildings, wondering what she found of interest here.

Once home for children sponsored by the Masons, the buildings had been vacant for years and decay had set in. The brick wall surrounding the property had crumbled, windows were broken, weeds and vegetation had taken over the landscape. It's haunted look gave substance to the scary stories children shared about the place. Despite the No Trespassing signs posted, teenagers used it as a meeting place to sneak a beer or a passionate ride in the back seat of their car with their sweetheart.

Callie was enchanted.

"Prudy would love this," she said, her gaze darting from one building to the next.

"Prudy?"

"A friend of mine in Dallas."

Judd leaned around her to look out the window, trying to see what she saw. "What's there to love?"

Callie looked at him in surprise. "Where is your vision? Your sense of adventure?" She turned back to the window. "Imagine how this must have looked when it was inhabited. How it could look with a little work."

"A *little* work?"

"Okay, a lot of work. But just imagine if the grounds were cleaned up, the building restored. It would be magnificent!"

"For what?"

Callie looked at him with an impatient frown. "I don't know! But something." She turned back to the window. "Prudy would know. She has vision."

Judd cranked the ignition, biting back a smile. "Right. Now what else would you like to see?"

She heaved a sigh as she continued to stare out at the abandoned buildings. "Your bedroom ceiling."

Judd whipped his head around. She turned and smiled sweetly at him. "You asked."

* * *

His place, as he'd called it that morning when he'd invited her to stay with him, consisted of acres and acres of rolling pastures sectioned off by black creosote fencing. Embedded in the limestone pillars flanking the entrance, black wrought-iron twisted to form the brand JB. Horses lifted their heads from their grazing as the truck passed, their ears pricked, watching. Delighted by the pastoral setting, Callie pressed her nose to the window.

Judd drove over a cattle guard, then the dam of a small lake where geese took flight at Baby's welcoming bark from the back of the truck. From there, the asphalt drive snaked its way up a small rise to end at a limestone ranch house.

Judd had bought the place when his career had first taken off. He'd remodeled the original house, added a wing that held a music room and a small theater. He'd cleared the land, built fences and barns, all for his own pleasure. Although he'd spent most of his time at his home in Nashville, through the years he'd always returned here to rest and regroup. It was his secret hideaway and to him this was home.

He stopped the truck in the circle drive in front and turned off the ignition. "Well, this is it." He threw an arm along the back of the seat, watching for Callie's reaction. He'd brought women here before, but he'd never particularly cared whether they'd like it or not. The tangle of nerves in his stomach told him that Callie's opinion was important.

Her face remained turned to the window, her gaze fixed on the long front porch where a willow porch swing moved gently in the wind. "I know this probably sounds silly," she said, embarrassed by the admission. "But I feel as if I've come home."

The knots in Judd's stomach slowly unraveled. He shifted to squeeze her shoulder. "You have. For as long as you like."

Callie twisted in the seat and met the warmth of his gaze. Unable to contain the happiness swelling in her heart, she threw her arms around his neck. "Judd Barker, you might regret saying that to me."

Closing his eyes against the sting of emotion, he hugged her back. "Not by a long shot, darlin'."

That first quick tour of Guthrie was the only glimpse of the town Callie saw for almost a week. Two people, holed up in a house with only each other for company, might have grown bored after a few days. Not Callie. And certainly not Judd. Their time together took on the quality of a honeymoon. Long nights of loving. Sleeping late of a morning. Relaxing strolls through the pastures with Baby trotting at their sides. Long, lazy soaks in Judd's hot tub. Meals shared across the kitchen table with Callie no farther away than the stretch of a bare toe.

He loved to watch her sleep, her body curled close to his. He loved to listen to her talk, no matter what the subject. She had a way of fluttering her hands when she became excited and her eyes would sparkle brighter than stars on a summer night. Her laughter filled his house with music and his heart with sunshine.

He tried hard not to think about the time when she'd leave, but the clock marking the time for the Houston hospital presentation ticked silently away. He'd find himself looking at her, already missing her vibrance and presence in his life. He wondered if she thought, too, about the time when she would leave, and called himself a fool.

Why would she want to stay with a washed-up singer like himself in a one-horse town like Guthrie? he asked himself more than once. Not that he'd trade Guthrie for any other spot in the world. Here he felt safe, protected from the ugliness he'd endured from the media during his trial.

No, he wouldn't leave Guthrie. And he couldn't ask Callie to stay.

"You're sure you want to have Thanksgiving dinner at my mother's?"

Callie rolled her eyes as Judd turned down a residential street. "You've asked me that twenty times, and my answer is the same. No, I don't mind."

He stopped in front of a house. "Well, I just want to make sure. She always has a house full of people, most of 'em strangers."

"Since I don't know very many people here, they'll all be strangers to me."

He turned off the ignition, obviously uncomfortable and wanting to say more. "Mother can be pretty nosey," he said slowly. "And bossy, too."

Callie laughed and reached across the seat to pat his arm. "You forget. I've met your mother. She's charming and sweet and polite."

Judd's mouth twisted sardonically. "Yeah, right." He shoved open his door and climbed out. "Just don't say I didn't warn you," he mumbled over his shoulder.

When Callie stepped through the front door of the Barkers' home, she immediately knew Judd's warnings weren't totally exaggerated. The house was full of people and most of them strangers. She was passed from one group to the next, exchanging names and pleasantries, and by the time she reached the kitchen where Molly was busy filling glasses, she was relieved to see a familiar face.

Molly grabbed a dishcloth to dry her hands and hurried over to give Callie a hug. "I'm so glad you could come," she said.

"Thanks for inviting me." Callie glanced around the crowded kitchen where counters were heaped high with food. "Is there anything I can do to help?"

"Yes," Molly said, slapping Judd's hand from a basket filled with rolls fresh from the oven. "You can supervise the carving of the turkey." She thrust a carving knife and fork toward Judd, then swept an apron around Callie's waist.

"And make sure more turkey goes on the platter than in his mouth," she said as she bustled away.

"I told you she was bossy," Judd mumbled, but dutifully positioned the knife and fork over the roasted turkey.

Callie pressed against his arm, watching while he sliced off a leg and set it aside. "Do you know what you're doing?" she asked dubiously.

He lifted his gaze to hers. "Would you like to do the honors?" he asked, offering her the fork and knife.

Callie stepped back, her eyes wide. "Heavens, no! I wouldn't know where to begin."

"You've never carved a turkey?" he asked in surprise.

She arched a brow. "I can go you one better than that. I've never seen a turkey carved."

"You're kidding."

"Nope. In fact, I don't remember ever seeing a whole turkey before. Our family always ate Thanksgiving dinner at the country club. The turkey was carved by the chef in the kitchen and served to us sliced on our plates."

Thanksgiving dinner at a country club. Judd couldn't imagine anything worse. Dinner served by waiters, moving silently and unobtrusively around the table. Everyone talking in low, polite voices. No laughing, no teasing, no stealing food from the kitchen when your mother wasn't looking. He didn't realize how lucky he was to have a mother who insisted on family traditions...or how deprived Callie was not to have had those same traditions.

He laid the knife and fork aside, gathered Callie into his arms and kissed her long and deep. When he drew away, she looked up at him, her eyes wide. "What was that for?" she asked breathlessly.

He turned away, picking up the knife and fork again. "Just my way of giving thanks."

With the Thanksgiving holiday behind them, the residents and businessmen of Guthrie turned their attention

toward Christmas. Decorations started popping up in stor
windows. The lampposts downtown were draped in green
ery and lights.

Though Judd would rather have kept Callie all to him
self at his ranch, he was determined to make good his pledg
that she see all the sights that Guthrie had to offer. To mak
sure she received a full education on Guthrie's history, h
planned another full day in town. He took her on a walkin
tour, serving as her private guide through the Territoria
Museum and the State Capitol Publishing Museum.

They walked the streets of Guthrie hand in hand, duck
ing into antique shops and browsing when they grew cold
They lunched at Granny Had One, dined on barbecue at th
Stables and had a beer with Hank at the Blue Bell Saloon.

After watching the evening performance of *Christmas o*
the Prairie at the Pollard Theater, Judd hired a horse-draw
buggy to drive them on a moonlit ride through the town
Carolers, dressed in period costumes, strolled along th
sidewalk, their harmonized voices filling the cold night ai
with the sounds of Christmas.

This was the Guthrie Judd loved. The peaceful streets, th
tranquil setting, that special magic unique to small towns
He looked at Callie, riding beside him, blankets pulled t
her chin, and wished this night could go on forever.

At that very moment, she tipped her face up to his, a
contented smile touching the corners of her mouth. "I lov
you, Judd Barker," she murmured before touching her lip
to his.

His heart twisting in his chest, Judd hugged her to him
wishing he could offer her the same words in return.

She touched a finger to his cheek as she withdrew. He
eyes filled with her love for him, she whispered, "Thank yo
for sharing Guthrie with me. It's a wonderful town."

Judd tucked her head beneath his chin. "Yes, it is," h
replied honestly, for with her there with him, it wa
true...everything was wonderful.

* * *

He was thinking about the moonlit carriage ride and Callie's profession of love when he walked in from the barn the next day and found her curled up on the den sofa, the phone tucked to her ear. She was laughing, her head thrown back, the phone cord braceleted around her wrist. She lifted a hand and waved, but kept right on talking.

He resented the invasion into their private time, as slight as it seemed. It was only a reminder that there was a world beyond the limestone pillars of his ranch, one in which Callie belonged . . . and he no longer did.

"Yes, you can tell John to make all the arrangements," he heard her say. "I'll drive home first, so he needs to make my flight reservations from Dallas." She laughed again, then said, "Yes, Prudy, I realize you're not my personal secretary." She listened a moment, smiling, then said, "Thanks, you're a doll." She stretched to replace the receiver, then held out a hand to Judd.

Instead of going straight to her, he shrugged out of his jacket. If she noticed his hesitation, she didn't show it.

With her hand still outstretched, she teased him with a smile. "Come here, you big lug, and give me a kiss."

He tossed his jacket across a chair and ambled her way. By the time he reached the sofa, he'd managed to put a halter on his selfish thoughts. "Who's John?"

"My agent."

"What flight is he arranging?"

"My trip to Houston. He wants me there earlier than we'd originally planned for some interviews."

Judd didn't want to ask, but he couldn't stop himself. "When do you leave?"

"I have to be in Houston on Friday, but I'll need to leave here tomorrow so I can drive home and pick up a few things."

Twenty-four hours, he thought, the muscles in his jaw tightening. Twenty-four hours and she'd be gone.

"Hey!" she said, tugging at his chin. "Why the long face?"

"Heck," he said, struggling to keep his voice light. "I was just gettin' used to you being under foot."

Callie laughed, bussing him full on the lips. "You sound as if I'm going away forever. It's just a trip. A business trip, and a short one."

Judd knew it was just a trip, a short one, but he couldn't stop the knot of fear that curled cold and hard in his gut. He knew that once she felt the excitement of the city and was surrounded by her friends and family, there was a possibility she might not want to come back. He knew this because he'd once felt the enticement of the city, the warmth of the spotlight and that heady sense of power that came with it. But he'd also experienced the other side of fame. The cold, bitter loneliness. The exposed feeling that came when your life was placed under a microscope for the entire world's inspection. He never wanted to experience that level of vulnerability again.

"Sure," he agreed, forcing a smile.

On sudden inspiration, she caught his hand in hers. "Come with me," she said. "It would mean so much to have you there when the statue is unveiled."

Judd's blood ran cold at the very thought. "No," he said as he rose, pulling his hand from hers. "I don't make public appearances anymore." He crossed the room, putting distance between them while he pulled a beer he didn't want from the refrigerator behind the bar.

Surprised by his refusal, Callie stared at his back. "But it's not a public appearance. Not for you, anyway." She rolled to her feet and crossed to him. "It's just a cocktail party and a brief presentation." She slipped her arms around his waist and pressed her cheek to his back. "I know it'll be boring, but I promise we'll stay only as long as required. Please say you'll come with me. Please?"

The swell of her breasts, the accompanying heat penetrating his shirt, the scent of wildflowers swirling beneath his nose all worked their own seductive power, making the fact that he hadn't made a public appearance in over a year dull in importance to his wish to please her, to be with her.

But then the memories came humming back. The crushing crowds, the blood-sucking reporters, the cameras flashing in his face, the damning headlines...the shame. He couldn't face that. Not again. Not even for Callie.

Twenty-four hours. That's all he had. He turned, catching her up in his arms. "I have a better idea," he suggested before stealing her breath with a kiss. "Let's make love."

Callie laughed. "Now? It's not even noon."

"So?" He lifted her higher, centering his mouth over a breast and teasing her with his tongue through layers of fabric.

"Now that you mention it," she whispered, intoxicated by the sensations flooding her, "a nooner sounds kind of nice."

Sleepily, Callie reached for Judd but found only cool sheets. Sitting up, she looked around the room where afternoon sunshine dappled the walls. Then she heard guitar music coming from the far side of the house. She sank back against the headboard, catching her lower lip between her teeth and the sheet beneath her chin, the distance he'd placed between them weighing heavy on her heart.

Something was changing between them, and for the life of her she couldn't figure out what or why. With each passing day, Judd grew quieter and more reserved. Sometimes she'd catch him watching her, his eyes filled with a sadness she couldn't explain.

She'd tried to overlook his moodiness, but earlier, when they'd made love, she'd sensed a desperation in his lovemaking that had never been there before. An urgency, a clinging as if this were their last time together.

She let her mind drift back to the conversation they'd had when she invited him to go with her to Houston. His refusal had been quick and final. And when she'd tried to persuade him to reconsider, he'd skillfully changed the subject by seducing her.

Though he shared his home and his bed with her, he apparently didn't want to share his life. She'd read enough about what happened to him during the trial to know that the accusations made against him had cut deeply, hacking away at his self-confidence and his pride. As a result, he'd obviously lost his ability to trust. Even her. And that hurt.

Plucking Judd's shirt from a chair by the bed, she stuffed her arms through the sleeves and climbed from the bed, determined to prove to him that he could trust her, not only with his life, but with his heart. She buttoned two buttons as she followed the sound of the music down the hall and wove her way through the country kitchen. A pair of paneled doors, which led to a wing of the house he'd told her he never used, stood partially open.

She slipped through and found Judd at the end of a long hall in a combination office and music room. He was sitting on the bench of a baby grand, dressed in nothing but jeans. The top three buttons of his fly were open, revealing a triangular patch of dark hair that disappeared in the folds of denim. The waist of his guitar rested on his thigh and his head was tipped to the fingerboard, his ear cocked and listening while his fingers moved deftly over the frets. His lips moved in the whispered lyrics of a song.

When he saw her, he flattened a hand against the strings, silencing the instrument.

She crossed to him, slipping onto the piano bench behind him. "Please don't stop, that's beautiful," she said.

"It's just a song," he said gruffly as he set the guitar aside.

That he wouldn't share his music with her was just another indication to Callie of all he held back.

Judd twisted on the bench until his knees bumped hers and their gazes touched. He saw the hurt in her eyes and knew he'd put it there. To ease it, he forced a smile as he caught the collar of the shirt she wore in his fingertips. "Nice shirt."

"I like it," she said stiffly.

His fingers skimmed lower, but she refused to be distracted from her purpose in seeking him out. Catching his hand in hers, she forced him to look at her. "Judd. What's wrong?"

He held the smile in place while he looked at her in puzzlement. "Nothing. Why?"

"I don't know, but you seem—distant," she said helplessly. "Have I done something or said something to anger you?"

He caught her face between his hands, his heart breaking at her distress. "No. I don't think you could. I'm just moody, is all." He brushed his lips over hers, then levered a finger beneath her chin, tipping her face up till their eyes met. "I'm sorry if I upset you. I didn't mean to."

She laid a hand over his. "You're sure?"

He grinned. "Positive."

Over his shoulder, she glimpsed a framed picture on the edge of the piano. She reached behind him and angled it for a better look. Her eyes widened and she lifted her gaze to his. "Dolly Parton?"

Judd glanced over his shoulder at the photo. "Yeah. That was taken at the Country Music Awards two years ago. We were presenters for Entertainer of the Year."

"Wow!" She let her gaze travel farther to the wall opposite her, noticing the framed pictures, the awards, the gold and platinum records displayed there.

She stood and crossed to stand before the wall of memories. Pictured was a side of his life she couldn't even imagine. Judd aligned with stars both new and old from the screen as well as the music world. Judd captured on the stage, his face contorted with emotion as he belted out a song.

She stared at the pictures of him, seeing the light in his eyes, the pure pleasure he got from entertaining, and wondered how he could have given it all up. "You love singing, don't you?"

"I did."

"You still do," she corrected, her back still to him. "And you miss it. I hear it in your voice and I see it in your face when you sing."

"You're wrong. I don't miss it."

"No, *you're* wrong, Judd," she said, turning and pointing her finger at him. "That's why you're here right now playing when no one else is around to hear. You do it at the Blue Bell. You do it here. But you won't share your music with anyone else. Not even me."

That he'd hurt her was obvious, but it couldn't be helped. Judd couldn't give her what she wanted. They'd stripped him of everything. His career. His name. His pride. All he had left was his music, and he kept that strictly for himself.

"Oh, Judd," she said, seeing the turmoil within him and knowing she'd been right. "You have a God-given talent. Don't let what happened keep you from doing what you were meant to do...what you enjoy."

"I'm doing exactly what I want," he said defensively.

"Living in Guthrie and running a saloon?"

The flash of hurt in his eyes had her rushing to kneel at his feet. "I'm sorry, Judd. I didn't mean that the way it sounded. I just want you to be happy, that's all."

Because he saw the truth of that in her eyes, he cupped the back of her head in his hand. "I've had my share of the spotlight, Callie. From Vegas to Nashville and every place in between. I'd be a liar if I told you I didn't get a thrill every time I stepped onto a stage, because I did, and at times I do miss it. But I discovered that fame has two sides. That darker side is a place I never want to walk again. I'm content with my life here. For me, that's enough."

"But not for me," she said, staring at him dully. "You won't share it with me."

He lowered his gaze and dropped his hands to curl them around his knees. His fingers dug into denim. "I didn't say that."

"But it's true, isn't it?"

Judd's mouth curved in a frown. He cocked his head to look at her. "Guthrie's a small town, Callie. You're used to Dallas and your life there."

"It's not Guthrie you're afraid of, Judd, not totally."

She watched the war of emotions raging within him, but she wouldn't back off. Not now when everything was at stake.

"Answer me, Judd. It's not just Guthrie, is it?"

"This is my home, Callie, my refuge," he said in a low voice. Though she could see how much the admission cost him, he continued. "Some say I'm hiding here, and maybe I am, but I would never ask you to do the same." When she would have denied his words, he tightened his fingers. "I'm only going to say this once, so hear me out. I love you, Callie. Enough to let you come and go, and enough to never ask you to stay and live in the shadow of my past."

He'd said he loved her for the first time, but the meaningfulness of the words were lost in the restrictions he placed along with them.

To argue was pointless, she could see that. Instead, she leaned into him, wedging herself in the V of his legs.

She touched her lips to his, withdrew slightly, then touched them again. Again and again she repeated the kiss, each time increasing the length and intensity, silently telling him that his past didn't matter while she attempted to soothe his fears with her hands.

"Callie," he whispered huskily. "I love you so much."

And she loved him, but knew words would never be enough to convince him. She'd have to prove her love to him. Her hands found their way to the fly of his jeans and she unbuttoned the remaining two buttons. Easing her hands around his waist, she worked the jeans down his hips and legs. After tossing them aside, she slowly moved to stand before him.

With her gaze on him, she slipped his shirt from her shoulders and let it drop to pool at her feet. She stepped out of it, then moved closer, offering herself in the most basic of ways. "And I love you, Judd," she murmured.

Hesitant at first, he reached for her breasts, taking them in his hands and gently drawing her to him. Bracing her hands on his shoulders, she straddled him while he closed his mouth hungrily over a breast.

His thighs burned hot against hers and the swell of his manhood curled hard and throbbing against her abdomen. She closed her eyes as arrows of desire shot through her to pierce that most secret part of her femininity. Wanting to please him as much as he always pleased her, she took him into her hand. A shudder quivered through him at her touch, then he relaxed on a groan of sheer pleasure.

She played her fingers up and down the swollen shaft, teasing him, wanting him. A bead of honey purled at its tip, and she took it on her fingertip and stroked it down, then up again, in a mindless game of seduction. With every touch, with every breath, showing him her love.

With his mouth closed around her breast, he caught her beneath her hips, lifting her, then slowly lowered her until she was impaled on the staff of desire she had created. On a strangled sob, she threw back her head, glorying in the feel of him buried deep within her. Then she moved against him, drawing him closer and closer to that point of highest joining.

His breath hissed through bared teeth as he arched against her. He cried out her name as he dug his fingers into her hips and spilled into her.

With her body pulsing against his, Callie melted against his chest. She held him against her, oblivious to the heat and stickiness of their joined skins as the tension gradually eased from him. "I love you, Judd," she whispered. "Please say you'll reconsider and go to Houston with me." She waited, hoping to hear those same precious words repeated to her and with them his agreement to accompany her to Houston.

His breath continued to blow warm at her neck, but he remained silent.

He still didn't trust her enough to give himself over to her completely.

Nine

His hands stuffed deep into his pockets, Judd stood in front of the plate-glass window of the Blue Bell, staring at the bleak sky overhead.

"You're going to wear a hole in that glass if you're not careful."

Judd turned to find Hank watching him. Embarrassed, he shrugged and moved away from the front window. "Just daydreaming."

"Never hurts a man to dream now and again." Hank hefted to the bar a tray of dripping beer mugs fresh from the dishwasher. He picked one up and began to dry it. "Callie gone?"

"Yeah, she left this morning."

"Guess it's kind of quiet out at your place, huh?"

Judd angled a hip onto a barstool, one side of his mouth curved ruefully. "Like a tomb."

Chuckling, Hank set the glass on the shelf and plucked another from the tray. "Amazing, isn't it, how much noise a woman can make?" He stuffed the cloth into the mug and gave it a hard twist. "Always yappin' and carryin' on from the time they get up of a morning 'til they go to bed at night. A man could go deaf trying to listen to it all."

"How would you know?" Judd teased. "You're a confirmed bachelor."

Hank snorted. "And that's why. Can't stand the noise."

Grinning, Judd picked a pretzel from the bowl and broke it in half. He leaned over and gave Baby the larger portion before popping the remaining piece into his mouth. At the dog's soft whine, he glanced back down. Baby was looking up at him, his ears drooping, his eyes filled with a sadness that mirrored Judd's own. Judd leaned down and scratched him behind the ears. "You miss her, too, don't you, guy?" he murmured in understanding.

Hank juggled a mug to keep from dropping it. "Miss her? Callie? Hell, she hasn't been gone more than half a day."

"We still miss her, though, don't we, boy?" Judd asked Baby. In reply, the dog whined low in his throat.

"Well, for heaven's sake!" Hank huffed in exasperation. "If you're that lovesick, you should have talked her into staying a while longer."

Judd curled his hand affectionately around Baby's ear, then let it drop as he straightened. "She had to go to the unveiling of that statue in Houston."

"Then why didn't you go with her?"

Judd shot him frown. "You know why."

Hank put the mug on the bar and slung the damp cloth over his shoulder. He hitched one hip higher than the other and laid his forearms on the bar. "You know, when you were a youngun, you were meaner than sin. Your daddy was always having to get you out of one scrape or another while your mama stood by wringing her hands. Didn't slow you down, though. You'd whip anybody who got in your way." He shook his head sadly. "In all the time I've known you, I've never seen you walk away from a fight."

"It's not a matter of fighting," Judd replied irritably.

"Isn't it? Looks to me like they've got you pinned to the floor and you're not doing a damn thing about it."

Sequins in every color of the rainbow caught the chandelier's light and danced its reflection around the walls. The rich, the famous and the wannabes gathered in the hotel's ballroom to celebrate the opening of the hospital's new wing. More comfortable in her studio than in a crowd, Callie stood in the bevy of well-wishers and elbow-rubbers, smiling, making small talk and wishing with all her heart Judd was with her. She needed his calming support.

"If you're ready, Miss Benson. It's time for the unveiling."

Callie glanced up to find the hospital administrator standing at her side, waiting. Slipping her hand through the crook of his arm, she smiled, her lips trembling at the effort. "Yes, I'm ready."

The crowd parted, allowing them a path to the raised dais in the center of the room where a round marble table held the draped statue. As they passed through the throng of people, Callie smiled and nodded as cameras flashed, capturing the moment for the benefit of the morning papers.

She took her place beside the statue and waited while the man raised the microphone. "Ladies and gentlemen, if I could have your attention, please . . ."

Judd stood at the fringe of the crowd, his back pressed to a marble column and his arms folded across his chest, silently cussing Hank. If it weren't for his bartender, he wouldn't be in Houston, Texas, tempting fate. Instead, he'd be at the Blue Bell sharing a beer with the regulars, or at home, sitting in front of a fire and rubbing Baby's belly.

He heaved a sigh. But no, he'd knuckled under, and now here he was holding up a column and trying his best to keep a low profile. So far, he'd succeeded at both. The column was still standing and no one had recognized him or so much as looked his way. Not even Callie.

He caught an occassional glimpse of her, though, in the continually shifting swarm of people around her. The top of her head, the glimpse of an emerald sequined shoulder, the graceful flutter of her hand in the air as she spoke. So far, she hadn't seen him. For the time being, he decided to keep things that way.

A camera flashed at his right and he flinched unconsciously. He glanced in that direction and saw that the camera was aimed at Callie, not at him. He breathed a sigh of relief and returned his gaze to Callie. She was on the arm of some gray-haired man now, moving through the crowd toward the dais. When they reached the platform, the guy picked up a microphone and said something into it, which only those within a foot of him could hear. Gradually the noise abated and the man's voice lifted above that of the crowd.

"If I could have your attention, please. We are here to celebrate the opening of the new women's pavilion at City Hospital. In conjunction with the opening, tonight we are unveiling the statue created by Callie Benson, which will be placed on a marble table in the reception area of that wing." He gestured for Callie to join him at the microphone. "It is my distinct pleasure to present to you, Miss Callie Benson."

Taking her place at his side, Callie glanced out across the sea of faces as she took the microphone. Judd was surprised to see that her hand shook.

"I want to thank you for the privilege of creating this statue." Her voice broke and she dipped her head, pausing until she was sure she could control the quiver in her voice. When she lifted her head again, her chin was set in determination. "In sculpting this piece, my hope was to reflect the essence of woman and of motherhood unbound by any sense of time. Every artist places a little bit of themselves in their work, and this statue," she said, crossing to it and touching the pewter satin that draped it, "is no exception. I've named it Lizzy's Legacy, in honor of my great-great-grandmother, one of the original settlers of the Oklahoma Territory. It was women like her, who shared her spirit of adventure and her strength of character, who helped settle this land. Without her influence, I never would have completed the project."

Setting the microphone aside, she took the corner of the cloth between her fingers and slowly pulled. The top of the woman's head appeared first, then the pewter satin slipped slowly downward, revealing a face, a bare shoulder, a breast. The crowd pressed for a closer look as the satin fell to puddle on the floor at the base of the table, baring the full statue. A soft *ahhh* of approval rose from the crowd.

Judd saw the relaxing of Callie's shoulders as she monitored the response of the audience and realized for the first time she'd doubted her own talent. He shook his head in amazement.

It took a while for the crowd to thin enough for him to approach Callie, but when he reached her side, he laid a hand on her shoulder. She turned his way, smiling. When she saw him, her mouth formed a soundless *oh*. Then she was in his arms, her hands clasped tightly around his neck.

"You're here," she whispered tearfully. "I can't believe you're really here." Abruptly she stepped from his embrace and framed his face with her hands, as if to assure herself that he was really there and not a product of her imagination; then she was in his arms again, laughing.

"They liked it," she whispered at his ear.

"They loved it," he corrected, taking her hands to hold her out in front of him. His own smile grew to match hers. "Did you expect less?"

Knowing what it had cost him to come and what his presence meant to her and to their future, Callie squeezed his hands. "I wouldn't allow myself to think beyond completing it."

"Callie, dear, I'm so sorry we're late."

At the sound of the voice, panic flashed in Callie's eyes. She tore her gaze from Judd's and turned to greet a middle-aged couple.

"Mother. Father. I'm so glad you could make it." She turned a dutiful cheek for her mother's kiss. "I'm sorry, but you missed the unveiling."

Her mother pouted prettily. "Oh, dear. And it's all Papa's fault."

Callie frowned. "Papa's?"

"Yes, the nursing home called just as we were preparing to leave, informing us that he'd taken a turn for the worse."

Callie's expression turned stricken. "Will he be all right?"

Frances patted her daughter's hand. "Nothing to fret about, dear. Probably just another of his childish cries for attention."

"But who's with him?"

"We engaged a private nurse to sit with him around the clock. But don't you worry about Papa. This is your party." Smiling, she lifted her head, looking around. "Now where is that statue of yours?" she asked. "Your father and I are anxious to see it." At that precise moment, the crowd shifted, creating a direct line between Frances and the statue. Her spine stiffened perceptibly and her facial muscles froze. She pressed a fragile hand to her throat and turned back to Callie. "How very... modern," she finished after searching for just the right word.

Callie felt the familiar sting of tears at her mother's obvious disapproval. "Thank you, Mother."

She felt Judd's fingers squeeze hers reassuringly as he moved into the circle. "If it wasn't already promised to the hospital, I'd buy it myself."

Grateful for his words of encouragement, Callie smiled up at him.

A slight frown deepened the wrinkles around Frances's eyes as she witnessed the exchange. "I don't believe we've been introduced," she offered politely.

"Mother, Father. I'd like you to meet a friend of mine from Guthrie, Judd Barker. Judd, these are my parents, Jonathan and Frances Benson."

Judd released Callie's hand to shake first one, then the other's hand. "A pleasure to meet you both," he murmured. "I'm sure you're proud of your daughter."

"Yes, we are," Mrs. Benson agreed, turning her head to steal another glance at the statue. Sighing, she turned back. "Though she might have clothed the woman and achieved the same affect."

"Did you say your name was Barker?" Jonathan repeated thoughtfully.

"Yes, sir."

"Any relation to the country-western singer?"

"One and the same."

Frances's lips pursed in disapproval as she raked him with a gaze, taking in the boots, the silver belt buckle, the bola. It was an effort, Judd could tell, but she managed not to curl her nose. The frown she wore suddenly vanished to be replaced by an engaging smile as she spotted someone she knew. "Oh, look, Jonathan. There is the mayor and his wife. We must say hello."

Frances hustled Jonathan away, and Callie looked up at Judd, her eyes filled with sympathy. "I'm sorry."

Judd slung an arm around her shoulders and hugged her tightly against his side. "Hey, the lady can't be all bad. She had you, didn't she?"

Callie looked up at him in surprise, then laughed.

"Did I hear you say you're Judd Barker?"

Callie and Judd both turned to find a man standing behind them. Judd struggled to hide his frustration at being recognized. "Yes, sir."

"I thought I recognized you. My grandson is a big fan of yours." The man patted his pockets, looking for something to write on. "Would you mind giving me your autograph for him?"

Judd accepted the paper and pen the man offered. "I'd be glad to." He turned Callie around to use her back as a writing surface. "What's your grandson's name?"

"Mickey."

Judd nodded and began to write. He thought he heard his name repeated, but wasn't sure. Then a camera flashed. Automatically, he threw up an arm to shield his face.

"Hey, Judd!" someone called. "Where you been hiding?"

Judd lowered his arm to frown at the man who'd shouted the question. "Around," he said vaguely.

The news of his presence skipped through the room like wildfire across a prairie. Some people began to stare, while the bolder ones moved in his direction. Reporters, scenting a story, pressed forward. Judd felt Callie ripped from his side. He watched in silent fury as the crowd pushed her farther and farther away from him while questions rang out, pelting him like a volley of gunfire.

"Could I have your autograph?"

"What are you doing in Houston?"

"Is Callie Benson your newest conquest?"

"Was the lady in Atlanta telling the truth? Did you rape her?"

"How does it feel to be an accused rapist?"

"How much did that not-guilty verdict cost you?"

"It was rumored that you had a nervous breakdown. Is it true?"

In the melee, he caught a glimpse of Callie's face. Her eyes were round in horror, her face ashen. This was exactly what he'd feared, what he'd wanted to protect her from.

Another camera was shoved into Judd's face. The flash went off, blinding him.

Outraged, he grabbed the camera strap and twisted until his fist lay just beneath the cameraman's chin. He shoved until the man was pressed against the marble column. Behind him more cameras flashed, pencils scratched, camcorders whirled, recording for posterity Judd Barker's reception back into the world he'd learned to hate.

Sickened by the vultures who continued to peck at Judd with their callous questions, Callie fought her way back through the crowd. She grabbed the hand of steel that held the strap twisted at the cameraman's neck.

"Judd, please," she pleaded. "Let him go."

When he didn't acknowledge her, she repeated, "Judd, please."

Slowly her words penetrated the anger and he loosened his grip. With a disgusted shove, he sent the man sprawling to the floor. Shaking free of Callie's hand, he turned and strode from the room without looking back.

Ignoring the questions hurled at her, Callie fought her way from the room and stepped onto the elevator behind Judd just before the door slid closed. Without looking at her, he slammed a fist against the button for the first floor and the car started a slow descent.

"Judd, I'm sorry," she began.

"It's not your fault," he said before she could say anymore. He lifted his gaze to the floor indicator. A muscle twitched on his jaw. "I shouldn't have come."

At the chill in his voice, fear rose in her throat. "You're leaving, aren't you?"

"Yes."

"Judd, please don't. You can't hide anymore."

"I'm not hiding."

"Running, then."

He refused to qualify her response with a reply.

She laid a hand on his sleeve. "Please, Judd. We can face this together."

He whirled, catching her by the elbows, his eyes blazing with fury. "Didn't you see what just happened?" he demanded, giving her a hard shake. "Didn't you hear what they said? I won't put you through that. Never again. I won't make you live under the shadow of my bad name."

The floor floated beneath their feet, signaling their arrival at the first floor. Callie stood staring at Judd, tears flooding down her face. "It doesn't matter, Judd, please," she begged. "Give us a chance."

"We never had a chance. They saw to that."

Helpless anger boiled up in her. "*They* didn't see to anything," she countered. "Oh, yes," she said, slicing the air with her hand when she saw his brow arch in surprise. "The media certainly did a good job on you during your trial. They were callous and rude and stuck their noses where they didn't belong. They printed half-truths and sensationalized the rest. But right or wrong, they were doing their job."

She poked her finger at his chest. "But *you* are the one who empowered them by accepting what they wrote about you. Until you face them, let the world see your innocence, they will continue to print their suppositions, and *you* will continue to live in the prison you've built around yourself." Her lip quivered and she lifted her chin. "I won't share that prison with you, Judd. It would destroy us both."

The door slid open with a quiet *shoosh*.

Emotion crackled between them in the heavy silence while Callie, her heart in her throat, waited for Judd to respond.

"Are you going up?" a gentleman asked timidly from the crowded foyer.

Judd released his grip on Callie and stepped back, his gaze fixed on her face. "The lady is," he murmured. "I've already been there and its a hell of a fall back down." He turned and strode away without looking back.

Unwilling to face the crowd of reporters in the ballroom again, Callie returned to her hotel room. Once there, she sank to the floor and buried her face in her hands, haunted by the look on Judd's face when he'd turned away. It was all her fault, she told herself. If not for her, he wouldn't have been there tonight. He wouldn't have been subjected to the cruel remarks, the probing questions, the nightmarish memories.

But couldn't he see what he was doing to himself? she raged inwardly. To them? What kind of future could they have together if he wouldn't let go of the past?

The phone rang and she lunged for it, sure that it was Judd.

"Judd?" she asked, frantically swiping the tears from her cheeks.

"No, it's your mother."

Disappointed that it wasn't Judd and knowing what was coming, Callie sank onto the bed.

"I've never been so humiliated in my life," her mother raged. "Fighting like common street people in front of everyone. It will be all over the morning papers. I hope this is a lesson to you, Callie. People of our position can never be too careful whom we choose as our friends. Public scenes such as the one we just witnessed are devastating to one's reputation and career."

Callie banded her forehead from temple to temple with tight fingers. "Mother, I don't need to hear this right now."

"No, I'm sure you don't," Frances snapped, then added crossly, "Papa's worse."

Callie's head came up and her hand dropped to her lap. "What?"

"We received the news when we returned to our hotel. They've transferred him to the hospital and placed him in intensive care. I thought I should let you know the nurse said he asked for you."

Without a word, Callie replaced the receiver. Papa. Her Papa. She had to see him before it was too late.

*   *   *

Callie hesitated in the doorway, daunted by the whoosh of the respirator and the click and whir of the heart monitor whose screen frantically sketched the slim hold Papa held on his life. She didn't want to go inside the dimly lit room, but knew she had no choice. She took one step, then another, forcing herself to cross to the bed. Tears burned behind her eyes as she stared down at Papa. When had he shrunk? she wondered, shocked by his appearance. A tall man, robust even in old age, he looked frail and shriveled in the narrow bed.

"Papa?" she whispered.

"I'm sorry, dear, but he can't hear you."

Callie twisted to see a nurse rising from the chair in the far corner. "Is he—" She swallowed hard, unable to complete the question.

"No, no." The nurse rose and came to stand beside Callie. "He suffered a stroke earlier this afternoon. By the time we reached the hospital, he had slipped into a coma." She laid a hand over Callie's and squeezed reassuringly. "You must be Callie."

"Y-yes," she stammered, her reply thickened by tears. "His great-granddaughter."

The nurse nodded, knowingly. "He said you'd come."

Grief welled in Callie's throat. "I just hope I'm not too late."

"I'm sure he draws comfort from your presence." She patted Callie's hand in silent understanding. "I'll just slip out to the nurse's station and leave the two of you alone. If you need me, press the buzzer."

Callie waited until the door closed behind the woman, then she scooted a chair next to the bed and sat down. She took Papa's hand in hers and nearly wept at the weightless fragility and the paper-thin skin.

"Papa? It's me, Callie. I came as quickly as I could." Not knowing what to say or even if he could hear her, she stumbled on. "I was in Houston at the presentation of my statue. I wish you could've been there. The statue turned out well. I named it Miss Lizzy's Legacy, for your mother. I hope you don't mind.

"She was the most wonderful woman, Papa. You'd have been so proud to have known her. I found the diaries she kept of her journey to Oklahoma. You were told she died giving birth to you, but that wasn't true. I'm not sure how or why, but you were taken from her, and she was told you had died. She never knew you lived, just as you didn't know she did."

She released his hand to dig the journals from her purse. "I brought them with me, her journals, so you could read them." She held them out, then slowly pulled them to her breasts, tears budding as she realized the chances of him ever accomplishing that feat. Not wanting to give in to the sadness, she struggled to think of something more cheerful to share with him.

"I wish you could've gone to Guthrie with me. It's such a wonderful little town." She sighed as her memories carried her back. "You can walk just about anywhere you want to go or there's a trolley you can ride to see all the sights. The whole community is devoted to restoring the old buildings and landmarks and preserving Guthrie's history. There's a saloon and a hotel that's been converted into a bed-and-breakfast and lots of good places to eat. Everyone is so friendly," she added, thinking of Molly, Frank and Hank.

She dipped her head and bit at her lower lip as memories of her last confrontation with Judd surfaced. Sniffing back the tears, she lifted her chin determinedly and reached out to touch Papa's hand. "I fell in love while I was there, and I know you'll be disappointed," she said, smiling through the tears, "but I won't be marrying Stephen." She knew if Papa were able he would hoot with laughter, for he'd always despised Stephen, referring to him as that "posturing peacock," both to his face and behind his back.

But he would've liked Judd. In some ways they were very much alike. Both with gruff exteriors but with the tenderest of hearts buried beneath. And both as stubborn as mules.

"He's the most wonderful man," she said wistfully. "Good and kind and handsome. His family owns a building that once belonged to your mother. Some of her trunks were there, and he gave me her journals to read." Reminded of the books, she opened one. "I want to read to you what she wrote about her journey to Oklahoma and your birth." She squeezed his hand. "I hope somehow you can hear me and know how much she wanted you and loved you."

Wanting Papa to know the truth about his mother and find peace, she read and reread each word, each page. As she read, she was reminded once more of the strength and spirit of the woman who'd written the words. Of all that she'd sacrificed for love, only to find that the man she'd entrusted with her heart was undeserving of such a prize. She relived the birth, grieved again with Lizzy at the loss of her son, and wondered anew about all the lost years. What would've happened if Papa had been raised by his mother? Would all their lives—hers included—have changed in any way? Would she have ever met Judd and fallen in love?

Love. She'd never really known the meaning of the word until she'd met Judd. She had no more doubts about the emotion, for as Miss Lizzy had promised in her dream, her heart had told her she was in love. The weight of it still pressed heavily against her chest even at the thought of Judd.

Throughout the next week, Callie never once left Papa's side. She slept in the chair beside his bed and ate only enough to satisfy the concerns of the private nurse. She read, she talked, she soothed, but throughout her vigil, he never once moved or spoke, nor in any way acknowledged her presence.

Just after midnight on the eighth day of her vigil, she propped the journal against Papa's hip, pillowed her chin in her hand and began to read, yet again. Within minutes, her eyes grew heavy and her head began to nod. Exhausted, she let her head drop to the mattress and she slept.

"Callie? Callie, come here, child."

She heard the sound of the raspy voice and thought she was dreaming.

"Callie. Callie, wake up."

She blinked open her eyes to find Papa looking at her, his hand outstretched.

Instantly awake, she grabbed for his hand. "Papa! Are you in pain? Shall I call the nurse?"

"No. No pain," he whispered. He wet his parched lips, then squenched his eyes. "The light is so bright. Can you see it?"

Puzzled, Callie glanced around the dimly lit room. "No."

Though feeble, he squeezed her fingers. "It's okay. I saw her, Callie. My mother. She told me you would come. Promise me you'll take me back to Oklahoma, Callie. Promise?" His eyes closed and his hand fell lax in her hand.

"Papa! Papa!"

The nurse heard Callie's frightened call and rushed back into the room. She wedged herself between Callie and the bed, forcing Callie out of the way, then took his wrist between her fingers. After a moment, she placed her cheek close to his mouth. She straightened, then pulled the sheet up over his face. "He's gone, Callie," she said gently.

The funeral was a trying affair. The family all gathered, pretending affection for a man they'd detested most of their lives. Each tried to hide their glee to at last be rid of him behind a solemn face. But Callie saw through the cheap veneer of their grief to the greedy hearts that lay beneath.

At Papa's request, and much to the outrage of his survivors, he was cremated. In his will, he requested that his ashes be scattered over his mother's grave in Oklahoma. Everyone was shocked and appalled by this request. Everyone except Callie. To her it was a fitting end. When she asked for the honor of scattering his ashes, no one denied her her request.

So it was on a cold December afternoon that Callie found herself once again entering Guthrie, passing along Division Street, turning right on Noble, then left on Pine. As she passed familiar landmarks, she looked neither left or right. She wouldn't let thoughts of Judd distract her from fulfilling Papa's request.

Within minutes, she passed through the limestone pillars marking the entrance to Summit View Cemetery. She parked near the Bodean plot, gathered the urn in her hands and slowly, reverently, walked to the graveside of Mary Elizabeth Sawyer Bodean. Standing in front of the granite marker, she stared until tears blurred the name. "I've brought him home to you, Miss Lizzy," she murmured softly. Taking the top from the container, she tipped the urn and slowly walked, letting the Oklahoma wind carry the ashes from Miss Lizzy's grave to that of her son's.

After replacing the urn's top, Callie knelt at the flat granite marker which had started her quest so many weeks before. She traced the familiar name, William Leighton Sawyer, then moved her finger down to trace the date of birth, June 14, 1890. Below it, just as she had requested, the date of his death had been carved. December 16, 1994. Only four days since his death, but it seemed like a year.

"Callie?"

At the sound of the familiar voice, she dropped her chin to her chest. She'd feared that she would run into Judd before she left town, and wished fervently that it hadn't been now, not when all her emotions seemed so close to the surface. "How did you know I was here?" she asked, keeping a neutral tone in her voice.

"Hank told me. He was at the gas station when you passed through town." He stepped closer and hunkered down beside her. Scuffed boots, a short column of starched denim, the always present black duster and Stetson hat. Her heart cried out to him, but she kept her lips pressed firmly together, knowing that whatever was offered, would have to come from him. She watched him pick up a blade of dead grass from the ground and silently shred it.

He lifted his head and squinted at the sun. "I'm sorry about your great-grandfather."

"Did Hank tell you about that, as well?"

"No. Henry, the mason who did the work on the stone for you, was in the Blue Bell last night. He told me."

"Word travels fast."

Judd shrugged. "Small town." He opened his hand and let the wind have the shredded grass. "Will you be staying long?"

"Just for the day," she said, knotting her hands into fists to keep from reaching out to him. "I have some business to take care of, then I'll be going back home."

"Oh." He sat a moment, staring at the ground, then picked up another blade and rolled it between the tips of his fingers. "The Historical Society's fund-raiser is tonight over at the Masonic Temple. If you decide to stick around, I could get you a ticket."

Callie turned to look at him, angered that he wouldn't address the issue directly. "Are you asking me to stay?"

For the first time since he'd approached her, he turned his head and looked at her full in the face. He knew what she wanted. The fact that he couldn't give her that cut him like nothing else had before. Impatiently, he tossed the grass blade to the ground, pushed his hands against his knees and rose. "I guess I better be going."

Callie ducked her head and swallowed back her grief. "Yes, I guess you'd better," she murmured.

"Molly?"

Startled, Molly whirled. A smile bloomed on her face as she hurried to the front door of the Harvey Olds House Museum. "Callie!" She grabbed Callie's hands in hers, then dropped them to gather her in her arms. "Oh, my, but it's good to see you."

She stepped back, holding Callie at arm's length, smiling like the sun had just come out after a long rain. "Have you seen Judd?"

Callie ducked her head to hide the trace of tears. "Yes, at the cemetery."

"At the cemetery?" Molly asked in surprise.

"My great-grandfather died. I brought his ashes to spread on Miss Lizzy's grave."

Molly drew Callie into her arms again. "I'm so sorry. I know how much he meant to you."

Callie sniffed, and Molly pulled a tissue from her pocket and pressed it to her hand, then led her into the parlor.

After sitting down on the settee, Callie shrugged her purse from her shoulder and dug into its depths. "I have your key." She passed the key to the whorehouse to Molly. "I want to thank you for allowing me to use the building."

"My pleasure, dear."

"And I was wondering..." Callie glanced up and her eyes filled with tears again. "If you don't mind, could I have Miss Lizzy's trunks that are stored up there?"

"Why, certainly! They're yours for the taking."

"I don't have room in my car to take them home with me today, but—"

"Home? You mean you're leaving so soon?"

"Yes. There's no reason for me to stay."

Molly shifted from the rocker to the sofa and drew Callie's hand into hers. "Oh, Callie. I had so hoped."

Callie nodded, blinded by tears. "Me, too."

"He loves you. You know that."

"Yes, I know. And I love him."

Molly's heart went out to Callie, for she knew how stubborn her son could be. "Why don't you stay?" she suggested hopefully. "Just for the night. You can go to the concert and drive home tomorrow."

Though tempted, Callie shook her head. "No. Really, I think it's best if I go now."

Molly pulled a strip of paper from her pocket and pressed it into Callie's hand. Closing Callie's fingers around it, she offered her a smile. "Here's a ticket. Just in case you change your mind."

By the time Callie left Guthrie, darkness had veiled the town in black velvet, the perfect backdrop for the red, green and white Christmas lights adorning the lampposts and lining the merchant's windows. She rolled down her window just enough to let the carolers' voices fill her car with the sounds of Christmas. Memories of her midnight buggy ride with Judd swept over her.

She knew he was somewhere near. Probably less than three blocks away at the Blue Bell. A part of her wanted to go to him, to talk to him, to try to persuade him to give their love a chance. The other part, the part that owned her pride, wouldn't allow it.

It took every bit of strength she had to keep driving down Division Street toward the interstate that would take her back to Dallas...and away from Judd. Dulled by her sadness, she took the exit to I-35.

Gradually she became aware of the number of headlights streaking past her, headed in the opposite direction. It took her a minute to figure out that they were all headed for Guthrie and the Historical Society's fund-raiser and an opportunity to see Casey Hibbard perform in person.

Tempted, she glanced at the ticket she'd tossed to the passenger seat, then tore her gaze away, tightening her hands on the steering wheel. No, she told herself. Seeing Judd again would only postpone and intensify the pain of letting go.

Ten

Judd didn't have time to think about Callie leaving or what a fool he was for letting her go—or rather he didn't allow himself the time. There was a stage to set up, equipment to move, a show to put on. There would be time enough for regrets later... a lifetime of it.

When he walked into the auditorium of the Masonic Temple, there were a few minutes of awkwardness as he'd expected. He knew all of Casey's band members and most of her crew—having worked with them all on more than one occasion over the years. Although they were all friendly, they tiptoed around him. Not that he blamed them. He'd left Nashville without a word to anyone, and the stories that had floated around after his departure were anything but flattering. Everything from "he'd been committed to an insane asylum" to "he had skipped the country." He hadn't bothered to deny any of them.

Although the crew members talked and joked while they worked, no one mentioned his trial or his disappearance from Nashville and the music scene. At least no one did until Casey showed up.

But when she entered the auditorium and saw him up on the stage, she let out a whoop that stopped everyone dead in their tracks.

"Well, if it isn't Judd Barker, alive and in person!" she yelled. "Heck, I thought you were either dead or locked up in some nuthouse." She stood with the length of the auditorium between them as if poised for a fight.

There was a stretch of silence so tense a tightrope walker could've walked it while everyone waited for Judd's reaction. His eyes narrowed in barely controlled anger as he was confronted with one more thing he'd lost . . . a friend.

When he'd left Nashville, he'd left behind more than just the reporters and a career. He'd left friends—people like Casey who'd shared his interests, his love for music. He couldn't blame any of them for abandoning him in his hour of need, for they'd all tried to offer their support. He was the one who had never returned any of their calls or letters. He was the one who had shut them out of his life along with the memories.

Casey continued to stand in the narrow aisle, her hands fisted on a waist a man could span between the width of his hands. Her stubborn stance told Judd she wasn't going to allow him to ignore her any longer.

A grin began to grow inside him. Leave it to Casey, he thought with a shake of his head, little bit of a woman that she was, to bring him to his knees.

"Judd Barker dead?" he responded lazily, crossing to the edge of the stage. "He's too ornery to die. But crazy?" He hopped down from the stage and strolled up the aisle toward Casey. "Now, that's still up for debate."

He stopped in front of her, mirroring her posture—hands on hips, eyes narrowed, chin tilted at a defiant angle. The grin she'd spawned within him grew until it erupted, curving at his lips and sparkling in his eyes.

Casey tossed back her head and laughed, that mane of red hair of hers flying. The tension in the room eased as crew members breathed a collective sigh of relief, then one by one went back to their work, leaving Casey and Judd alone to talk about old times.

At the first strummed chord from the lead guitarist, the audience went wild. By the time the fiddler joined in, toes were tapping, hands clapping and hips moving to the country beat. Their enthusiasm pumped through Judd's veins. He loved a good show, loved the music, the audience; even fed off them when it had been him up on the stage. His fingers knotted in the stage curtains. God, how he missed it.

But this is Casey's show, he told himself, not mine. His job here was merely that of a member of the stage crew, making sure the lights, the sound system and the special effects for the show all worked without a glitch.

The band was doing their job, warming up the audience for Casey's appearance. Judging by the crowd's response, they didn't need much encouragement. Judd saw Casey weaving her way through the tangle of backstage crew and snakes of electrical cables. That trademark smile of hers flashed as she teased with the crew members, letting off a little of the nervous energy that every performer carried with them to the stage.

Judd felt a stab of envy, even a little regret, that it was her going on stage and not him. Shaking off the feelings, he held out the cordless microphone and forced a smile. "Ready?"

"You bet," she replied, curling her fingers around the mike. "Sure you won't join me?"

Judd shook his head. "Not this time." He guided her to the back of the stage, clearing a way through the black drapes that were part of the set. After helping her up to the top of a platform, he shot her a wink. "Have a good time."

"Always," she murmured, her concentration already focused on the choreography and the music as she awaited her cue.

Callie sank into the empty front-row seat next to Judd's mother, her breathing ragged, her heart thudding. She'd gotten as far as Norman, Oklahoma, before she'd convinced herself that Lizzy Bodean wasn't the only member of the Sawyer family with courage enough to withstand a little opposition. When she'd decided that, she'd thrown her pride out the window and caution to the wind, and headed back for Guthrie and one more chance with Judd.

Seeing Callie, Molly immediately reached for her hand and pressed a shoulder to hers in a gesture of support. "I'm glad you're here," she whispered. Before she could say more, the lights in the auditorium faded and the black curtain on the stage turned translucent to reveal the members of the band split by a staircase that climbed into the darkness. The music started softly, building in tempo and volume, while colored lights bled from one rich hue to the next. Smoke rose from the top of the stairs and lights pumped up until the silhouette of a woman appeared. A spotlight hit her and she lifted her head. Casey Hibbard. Callie fell under her spell.

With the performance drawing to an end, Judd edged his way to stand behind the backdrop of curtains. From his secluded position, he watched Casey move across the stage as she worked the audience, making sure that everyone felt a part of the show. He knew the energy required in putting on a concert like this and marveled at how easy Casey made it look. She was the ultimate entertainer, knowing how to work an audience, how to pull every bit of emotion from them. In return, she gave them one hell of a show.

His gaze drifted across the auditorium from the floor to the highest balcony, noting that the concert was a sellout.

The funds raised would enable the Historical Society to progress even more quickly with their plans for Guthrie's restoration. In so doing, they would capitalize on some of Oklahoma's tourist trade, creating jobs for Guthrie residents and attracting new business to the area. That he was a part of that effort filled him with pride, for it was one more step in fulfilling his debt to his hometown.

He turned his gaze to the front row reserved for members of the restoration group who were responsible for tonight's success. Myrna, Gertie, Eddy, his mother. They'd all worked hard to put together this fund-raiser. Even more would be required of them now to put the funds to good use. But what a difference it would make for Guthrie.

Applause erupted as the song ended, interrupting his thoughts. He chuckled when he saw his mother stick her fingers between her teeth and let out a shrill whistle. He'd seen her do that very thing when he'd been on the stage. She'd been so proud of him, so supportive while he'd struggled his way to the top of the country charts. She'd never once condemned him or doubted him, she'd just offered her unqualified love. While he continued to stare at her, regret swelling in his chest for all the mud that had been slung on their name, Molly turned in her seat and grinned at the woman next to her. Judd's heart stopped when he saw the woman's face.

Callie.

"Oh, God," he whispered under his breath. Before he could decide to run or stand, Casey was beside him, breathing hard and blotting the perspiration from her face. "Whew!" she sighed. "What a crowd!"

His heart felt as if it were being ripped in two, yet Judd kept his emotions from showing as he nodded toward the audience. They were on their feet, clapping wildly and shouting for more. "I think they want to hear another one."

Casey beamed. "My pleasure."

Before Judd knew what was happening, she had him by the hand and had lifted the mike. "Look who I found hiding backstage," she called to the audience as she dragged him back on stage with her. If possible, the applause and shouting rose in intensity.

"How would y'all like Judd and me to sing one together?"

The crowd went crazy, stamping their feet and shouting.

Judd tugged at his hand. "No, Casey. I can't."

She shook her head, keeping her gaze on him as she turned the mike to her mouth. "I can't believe this, but I think he's going to need some persuading." She cut a conspiratorial look at the audience. "Can you help me out?"

The cry started from somewhere in the back and rolled forward, building to a deafening roar. "We want Judd! We want Judd!"

Fear coiled in his stomach as he looked out at the audience. He couldn't sing. Not now. Not ever.

But then he saw Callie, sitting beside his mother, her hands pressed against her lips, her eyes wide and filled with hope. She'd said she loved him, and he believed her. She'd also said she wouldn't live in the prison he'd created for himself. He believed that, as well. He was getting a little tired of those walls himself.

Callie wanted it all or nothing. As he looked at her, he knew he was prepared to give her everything for one more chance at her heart. Praying that his offer didn't come too late, he swallowed hard and turned to Casey, giving her a tight nod.

Laughing, Casey waved a hand in the air to quiet down the crowd. "I believe we've talked him into it." She turned to the band. "How about 'Islands In The Stream'?"

A few chords were strummed while a band member passed Judd a mike. He accepted it reluctantly, testing its weight in his hand as he let the familiar equipment work its own form of comfort.

The first chords of the lead-in pulsed around him, and Judd's mouth went dry. He feared that when he opened his mouth to sing, not a sound would come out. He glanced at Callie and their gazes touched and meshed. The love in her eyes and her belief in him electrified him with a sense of power he hadn't experienced in over a year. He closed his eyes and let the music take him.

"Baby, when I met you there was peace unknown
I set out to get you with a fine tooth comb
I was soft inside, there was something going on"

His words were shaky at first, but grew in strength and emotion as the crowd welcomed him back.

Casey stepped next to him, twining an arm at his waist as she joined her voice with his.

"You do something to me that I can't explain.
Hold me closer and I feel no pain..."

A smile slowly built on Judd's face as he sang the words, letting the lyrics and the music free him from the memories and the fears. The song might have been written especially for him, they depicted his feelings for Callie so well. She did something to him that he couldn't explain, and it was while in her arms that he felt no pain.

At the end of the song, Casey threw her arms around him and gave him a big hug, laughing. The crowd went wild, clapping and stamping, demanding more. With a wink, Casey strolled past him, saying, "You're on your own now, cowboy."

On his own? Not anymore, Judd told himself. Not if Callie had meant what she'd said.

He picked up a guitar and dragged a stool to the center of the stage. Pulling the guitar across his lap, he strummed a few chords, his head tipped to the frets.

At the sound of the melody, shivers crawled up Callie's spine. It was the song she'd heard him play at the Blue Bell and again at his house, and though she recognized the melody, she'd never heard the lyrics.

One of the stage crew ran on stage to set a microphone in front of him and adjusted the height, then disappeared from sight. Judd hummed a few bars, then opened his mouth and let the words flow from his heart.

Tears burned Callie's throat and behind her eyes. She sat with her fingers pressed against her lips and listened as Judd musically told the story of what he'd been through, sharing the emotions in such a way, she felt his anger, his disillusionment and his shame as if it were her own. By the time he sang the last chorus, there wasn't a dry eye in the house.

> "This prison it holds me, built
>   one lonely brick at a time
> No more sunshine, no more laughter
> Just the walls of my prison
> And the ashes once my dreams..."

After the last chord faded, Judd hooked his bootheel over the stool's rung and propped the guitar on one knee. He lifted his head and looked out over the audience. No one applauded. No one cheered. They all looked at him, watching expectantly, as if they somehow knew there was more of the story to come.

"All of you know about the accusations and the charges filed against me," he said, his voice amplified by the microphone, but low and uncertain. "And even though the judge issued a verdict of not guilty, there are those who still believe I'm guilty." A cry of denial rose from the audience. Judd held out a hand to quiet them and sadly shook his head. "I've heard all the stories. Some say I bought my freedom by paying off the judge and jury. Others think I had a nervous breakdown after the trial and ended up in some insane asylum weaving baskets. The truth is...I came home.

"The song I just sang, I wrote after the trial. It was a hellish time in my life, something I wouldn't wish on my worst enemy. The one thing that kept me going during all of it was knowing that when it was over, when my innocence was proven, I could come home.

"Unfortunately, just having a judge proclaim me innocent didn't seem enough. The media continued to hound me, building suppositions on half facts, sniffing around for a story that just wasn't there. So, even though I'd come home, I realized that I hadn't truly escaped it all. I'd built my own prison, one lonely brick at a time, by avoiding talking about what happened. A friend of mine—" He stopped, frowned, then shook his head, chuckling. "Hell, she's more than a friend." He stood and set the guitar aside.

Callie's heart crawled up her throat as she watched him walk to the edge of the stage and stop in front of her. He held out his hand, palm up. She looked at Molly, not sure what Judd was asking of her. Molly just smiled and gave her a gentle shove. "Go on," she whispered.

Slowly, Callie rose and crossed to him, her knees knocking uncontrollably. With her gaze fixed on his, she laid her hand in his. He guided her up the two steps that separated them until she stood at his side.

He kept her hand in his as he looked out at the audience. "A year ago, the chances of Callie and I ever meeting were probably a million to one, what with her living in Dallas and me traveling all over the country, singing. If I hadn't been accused of a crime, I'd probably still be out there singing and partying and carrying on. I wouldn't have moved home to Guthrie and been here when Callie's great-grandfather sent her here to trace some of his family. You can call it fate, you can call it the work of God's mysterious hand, but whatever the reason, going through what I did was worth all the pain and suffering," he said, turning to look down at her. "For the opportunity to meet this special lady."

Tears burning her eyes, Callie stepped into the curve of his arm and laid a hand against his chest. The pounding of his heart beneath her palm matched the thunderous beating of her own.

He squeezed her against him, his gaze on her. "Callie convinced me that the only way to break out of this prison I created around myself is to go public, to set the story straight. She said we could face this together and I'm taking her at her word."

He shifted nervously, not wanting to broach the subject he'd avoided for over a year. He lifted his head, his chin held high as he stared out over the audience. "I'm not guilty of the crime I was charged with," he said. "And I didn't pay off anybody to reach that verdict."

The applause started immediately and built to a deafening roar as one by one the audience rose to their feet, showing their belief and trust in him. That they would accept him so readily with nothing but his own word as proof freed Judd as no judge's verdict ever could. He heaved a long sigh as the burden he'd carried for over a year slipped from his shoulders.

"To put a few rumors to rest," he said, beginning to relax, "I'm not on leave from some mental institution and I didn't skip the country. And I'm sure as hell not dead."

The crowd hooted with laughter at that last one.

"I'm alive and well and living in Guthrie, Oklahoma, and if this lady'll say yes," he said, looking down at Callie, "I plan to increase the population of Guthrie by one just as soon as I can find a justice of the peace who'll marry us."

A cheer went up as the crowd shouted their approval. Tears blinded Callie as she gazed up at Judd and saw the uncertainty in his eyes. Her heart filled with her love for him, she slipped into his arms and wound her arms around his neck. "I love you, Judd Barker."

"And I love you." Closing his eyes, he hugged her to him "No more prisons, Callie," he promised in a whisper "Never again."

*   *   *   *   *

Take 4 bestselling love stories FREE

Plus get a FREE surprise gift!

Coming in April from

SILHOUETTE®

Desire®

FROM HERE TO MATERNITY

THE PERFECT FATHER
by Elizabeth Bevarly

The latest book in her delightful series celebrating the unexpected joys of motherhood—and fatherhood!

Irresistible Sylvie Venner decided that confirmed bachelor Chase Buchanan was the perfect candidate to father her baby. Unfortunately, handsome and hardworking Chase had no plans of ever becoming a dad!

FROM HERE TO MATERNITY: Look what the stork brought—a bundle of joy and the promise of love!

SILHOUETTE® Desire®

Opposites Attract

A new series from Nancy Martin

Who says opposites don't attract?

Three sexy bachelors
should've seen trouble coming
when each meets a woman
who makes his blood boil—
and not just because she's beautiful....

In March—
THE PAUPER AND THE PREGNANT PRINCESS (#916)

In May—
THE COP AND THE CHORUS GIRL (#927)

In September—
THE COWBOY AND THE CALENDAR GIRL

Watch the sparks fly as these handsome hunks fall for
the women they swore they didn't want!
Only from Silhouette Desire.

DREAM WEDDING
by Pamela Macaluso

Don't miss JUST MARRIED, a fun-filled series by Pamela Macaluso about three men with wealth, power and looks to die for. These bad boys had everything—except the love of a good woman.

***

"What a nerd!" Those taunting words played over and over in Alex Dalton's mind. Now that he was a rich, successful businessman—with looks to boot—he was going to make Genie Hill regret being so cruel to him in high school. All he had to do was seduce her...and then dump her. But could he do it without falling head over heels for her—again?

Find out in DREAM WEDDING, book two of the JUST MARRIED series, coming to you in May...only in

Five unforgettable couples say "I Do"... with a little help from their friends

Always a Bridesmaid!

Always a bridesmaid, never a bride...that's me, Katie Jones—a woman with more taffeta bridesmaid dresses than dates! I'm just one of the continuing characters you'll get to know in ALWAYS A BRIDESMAID!—Silhouette's new across-the-lines series about the lives, loves...and weddings—of five couples here in Clover, South Carolina. Share in all our celebrations! (With so many events to attend, I'm sure to get my own groom!)

In June, **Desire** hosts
THE ENGAGEMENT PARTY by Barbara Boswell

In July, **Romance** holds
THE BRIDAL SHOWER by Elizabeth August

In August, **Intimate Moments** gives
THE BACHELOR PARTY by Paula Detmer Riggs

In September, **Shadows** showcases
THE ABANDONED BRIDE by Jane Toombs

In October, **Special Edition** introduces
FINALLY A BRIDE by Sherryl Woods

Don't miss a single one—wherever Silhouette books are sold.

Silhouette® ™

AAB-G

CODE NAME: DANGER

Because love is a risky business...

Merline Lovelace's "Code Name: Danger" miniseries gets an explosive start in May 1995 with

NIGHT OF THE JAGUAR, IM #637

Omega agent Jake MacKenzie had flirted with danger his entire career. But when unbelievably sexy Sarah Chandler became enmeshed in his latest mission, Jake knew that his days of courting trouble had taken a provocative twist....

Your mission: To read more about the Omega agency.

Your next target: THE COWBOY AND THE COSSACK, August 1995

Your only choice for nonstop excitement—

MAGGIE-1